"...That is not a sunset..."

Alice § An Integrity Knight of the Underworld and the world's first true bottom-up artificial intelligence. In *ALO*, she takes the form of a cait sith in the hope of becoming a dragoon.

"Kirito, l-look...!"

Asuna § Kirito's girlfriend. In *ALO*, she plays an undine magician and fencer.

Is that going to happen all over again?

Kirito § The boy who beat *SAO* and brought peace to the Underworld. In *ALO*, he plays a spriggan magic swordsman.

"Maybe it's an event battle."

Lisbeth
The girl who forged Kirito's swords in both *SAO* and *ALO*. In *ALO*, she plays a leprechaun blacksmith.

If I lose 30—no, 20 percent of my HP, I'll resign from the fight.

Silica
A girl Kirito saved in *SAO*. In *ALO*, she plays a beast-taming cait sith character.

"Good luck!"

Yui
Originally a mental health counseling program from *SAO*. The greatest top-down A.I. in the world.

"ⵏⵏⵏⵏ, ⵏⵏⵏⵏⵏⵏ."

Yzelma § An NPC warrior who speaks a different language from the players. Leader of the Bashin tribe's camp.

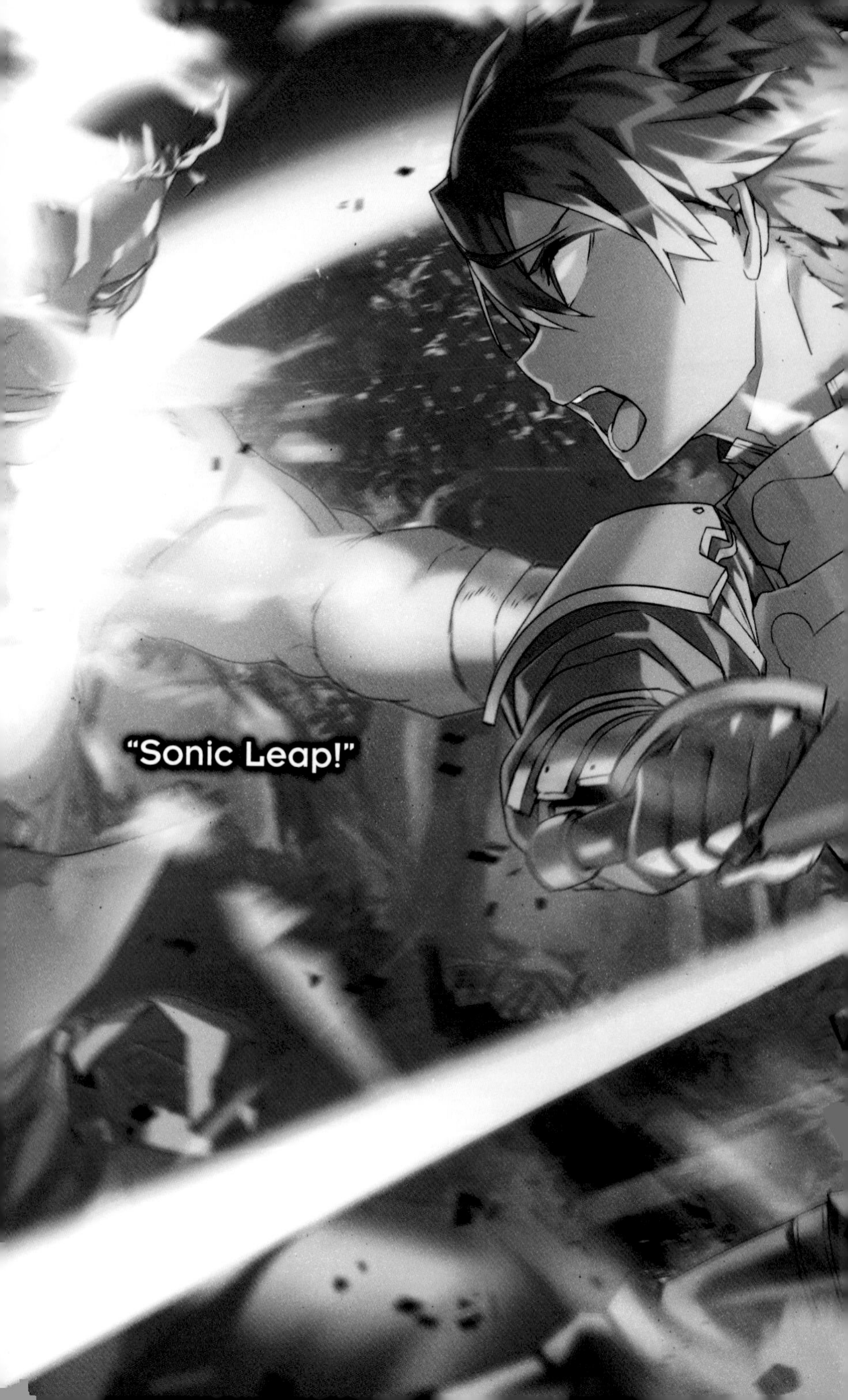
"Sonic Leap!"

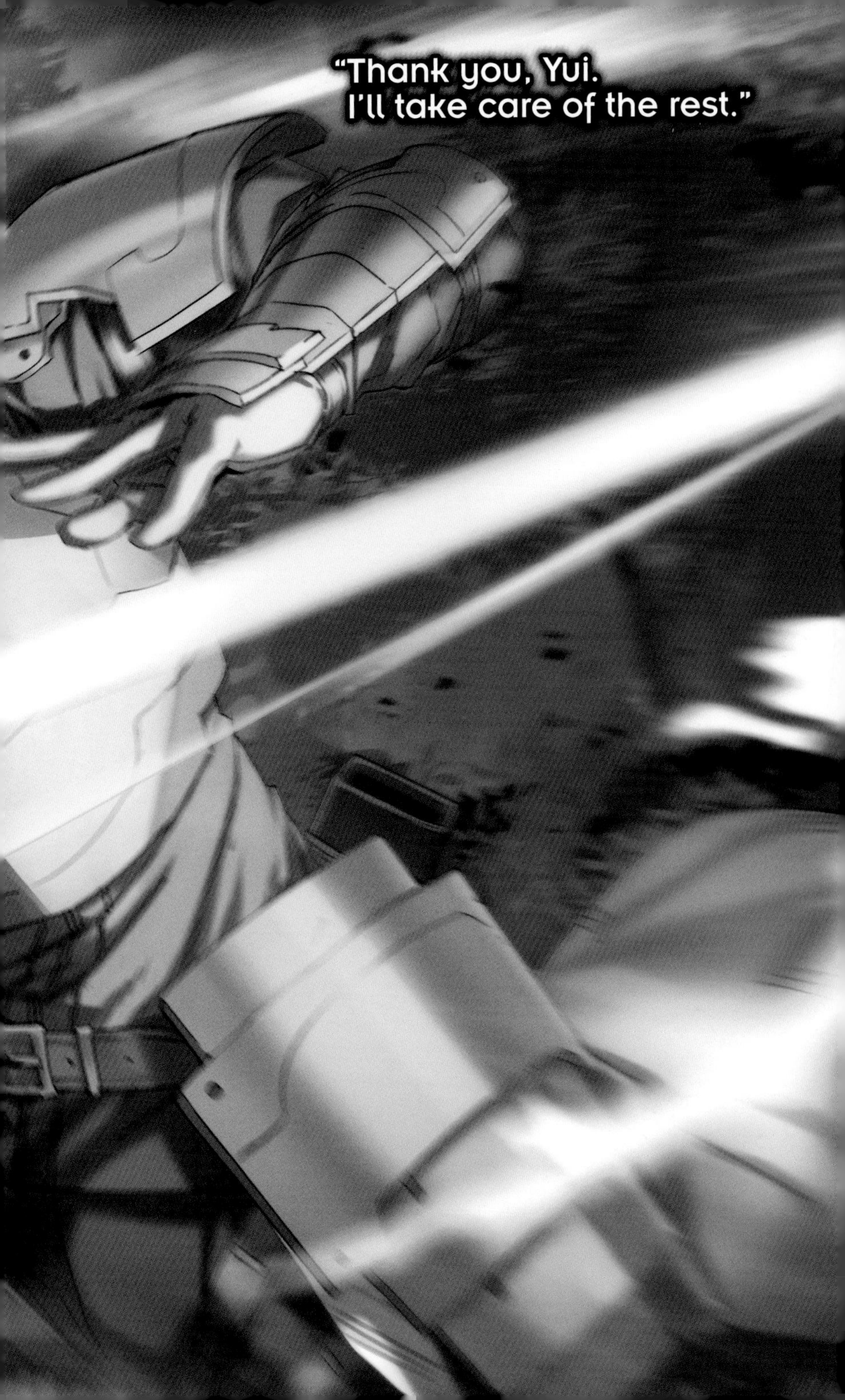
"Thank you, Yui.
I'll take care of the rest."

Unital Ring Outskirts Map
(Partial)

Log Cabin Landing Point

Giyoru Savanna

Zelletelio Forest

Bashin Basin

Battranka Highlands

Aincrad Landing Point

Jiruldera Plains

Stiss Ruins

Unital Ring is an open-world survival game shrouded in mystery. All you can bring from your pre-fusion game are your two weapons with the longest usage times, one skill with the highest proficiency level, and your currently equipped armor. Everything else, including player stats and items, is completely reset.

In terms of gameplay, it adds a player-level system that did not exist in *ALO* and the parameters of TP (thirst points) and SP (stamina points). If TP or SP gets to zero, HP will begin to decrease. Therefore, managing TP and SP will be a crucial and difficult task.

VOLUME 21

Reki Kawahara

abec

bee-pee

YEN
ON

NEW YORK

SWORD ART ONLINE, Volume 21: UNITAL RING I
REKI KAWAHARA

Translation by Stephen Paul
Cover art by abec

SWORD ART ONLINE Vol.21
©Reki Kawahara 2018
Edited by Dengeki Bunko
First published in Japan in 2018 by KADOKAWA CORPORATION, Tokyo.
English translation rights arranged with KADOKAWA CORPORATION, Tokyo, through Tuttle-Mori Agency, Inc., Tokyo.

English translation © 2021 by Yen Press, LLC

Yen On
150 30th Street, 19th Floor
New York, NY 10001

Visit us at yenpress.com
facebook.com/yenpress
twitter.com/yenpress
yenpress.tumblr.com
instagram.com/yenpress

First Yen On Edition: January 2021

Yen On is an imprint of Yen Press, LLC.
The Yen On name and logo are trademarks of Yen Press, LLC.

Library of Congress Cataloging-in-Publication Data
Names: Kawahara, Reki, author. | Abec, 1985– illustrator. | Paul, Stephen, translator.
Title: Sword art online / Reki Kawahara, abec ; translation, Stephen Paul.
Description: First Yen On edition. | New York, NY : Yen On, 2014–
Identifiers: LCCN 2014001175 | ISBN 9780316371247 (v. 1 : pbk.) |
    ISBN 9780316376815 (v. 2 : pbk.) | ISBN 9780316296427 (v. 3 : pbk.) |
    ISBN 9780316296434 (v. 4 : pbk.) | ISBN 9780316296441 (v. 5 : pbk.) |
    ISBN 9780316296458 (v. 6 : pbk.) | ISBN 9780316390408 (v. 7 : pbk.) |
    ISBN 9780316390415 (v. 8 : pbk.) | ISBN 9780316390422 (v. 9 : pbk.) |
    ISBN 9780316390439 (v. 10 : pbk.) | ISBN 9780316390446 (v. 11 : pbk.) |
    ISBN 9780316390453 (v. 12 : pbk.) | ISBN 9780316390460 (v. 13 : pbk.) |
    ISBN 9780316390484 (v. 14 : pbk.) | ISBN 9780316390491 (v. 15 : pbk.) |
    ISBN 9781975304188 (v. 16 : pbk.) | ISBN 9781975356972 (v. 17 : pbk.) |
    ISBN 9781975356996 (v. 18 : pbk.) | ISBN 9781975357016 (v. 19 : pbk.) |
    ISBN 9781975357030 (v. 20 : pbk.) | ISBN 9781975315955 (v. 21 : pbk.)
Subjects: CYAC: Science fiction. | BISAC: FICTION / Science Fiction / Adventure.
Classification: pz7.K1755Ain 2014 | DDC [Fic]—dc23
LC record available at https://lccn.loc.gov/2014001175

ISBNs: 978-1-9753-1595-5 (paperback)
          978-1-9753-1596-2 (ebook)

10 9 8 7 6 5 4 3 2 1

LSC-C

Printed in the United States of America

"THIS MIGHT BE A GAME, BUT IT'S NOT SOMETHING YOU PLAY."

—Akihiko Kayaba, *Sword Art Online* programmer

SWORD ART Online
unital ring I

Reki Kawahara

abec

bee-pee

> It never fails to be a wonder, speaking with you, now that you are so much older than me.

> Well, time might as well not exist to you now, isn't that right? As long as the hardware resources exist, your thinking can be as dense and fast as you want it to be.

> Theoretically, yes, but in practice, it is not so simple. Nearly all the supercomputers in the country are under *her* supervision now.

> Ah, I see. How ironic. The program you created and scrapped of your own volition is the force that now threatens you.

> On the contrary, it is a joy to me. The little seed I planted found purchase in distant networks, where it sprouts its own leaves and branches…Just conjuring the vision brings back many feelings I thought I'd lost with my physical body.

> You might not be human anymore, but you're still a romantic, I see. Then…what about the endless worlds that sprouted from the other seed you gave me…no, gave "him"? Are you satisfied playing the role of observer?

> I am leaving the future of The Seed Nexus to the will of the world itself and to the choices of all those who live within it.

Either they will expand without order and eventually wither away…or they will proceed to the next step, to Unification. And I do not know which it will be.

> Unification, eh? Even that might be…Actually, I'd rather not leave the rest of that statement in the log. I suppose I'll take a page from your book and watch what unfolds for a while.

1

My name is Kazuto Kirigaya, and I was born on October 7th, 2008…as far as I know.

This year is supposedly my eighteenth on this planet, and yet I don't feel entirely connected to that fact. Perhaps that's because I have absolutely no memory of my birth parents, who died when I was still a baby.

My birth father's name was Yukito Narusaka. My birth mother's name was Aoi Narusaka. If it hadn't been for the car accident that took their lives and gravely injured me, I would have grown up with the name Kazuto Narusaka. Maybe my online nickname would have been Naruto instead of Kirito—but I can't be sure of that.

For one thing, my interest in computers came from Midori, the mother who raised me, and my addiction to online games was in no small part a result of my loss of self-identity after learning I was a foster child. Perhaps Kazuto Narusaka would have grown up without any interest in computer games at all and never gotten stuck in the *SAO* Incident. At this point, such conjecture is pointless.

At any rate, ever since I peered at my national ID information when I was ten and learned the truth, I had a hard time feeling a true connection to my birthday. When I was in my second year of middle school, at my most rebellious stage, I refused to celebrate it at home and ended up making my adoptive sister, Suguha, cry.

Now, of course, I regret being so foolish, and last year's birthday was quite a big celebration, given that the previous two had happened in Aincrad. But even then, I could not fully accept the reality that I was born on October 7th. Most likely, that feeling would last until I knew everything there was to know about my birth parents.

And now my birthday was coming around again, in just ten days. When I turned eighteen, I would be allowed to get a driver's license and exercise my right to vote. Suguha was apparently making arrangements for a party; I was under strict instruction to return home immediately after school that day, and I was looking forward to it. But at this point in time, I had no leeway to think about my own birthday.

Because one week before that, on September 30th, just three days from today, was Asuna's birthday.

"Papa, have you decided on what you'll be giving Mama for her birthday?" asked the little fairy sitting on the rim of my mug.

I was leaning against the back of my mesh desk chair. "I haven't. I'm still thinking about it…"

The little fairy sounded less like a child and more like an older sister when she scolded, "Whether you're going to buy it at the store or order it online, it's not going to be in time if you don't decide soon. I wouldn't recommend the tightrope schedule you opted for last year, when you had to use your lunch break on the big day to pick it up!"

"I'd rather avoid that feeling of terror, too, but it's just really hard! Asuna never talks about how she wants this or that…Yui, do you think you could find a way to ask her what she wants?"

Yui, the artificial intelligence we met in *SAO* and had adopted as our daughter, was not having it. "You can't cheat like that! Mama will love anything you get for her, as long as you choose it yourself!"

"Yeah, I know that's true as a general rule, but…," I said, trailing off.

For her birthday last year, after much hemming and hawing, I finally settled on a red scarf for Asuna. I had decided on that because Asuna had a ninety-minute commute to school, which I thought would be very harsh on her in the middle of the winter. She did indeed wear it all through November to February, but the truth was, Asuna had enough scarves that she could tie them all up and play a giant game of jump rope with them. Surely some of them had better protection against the cold, too…but I only realized that after the worst of the winter was over.

So this year, I wanted to get away from practical items, but that was getting into territory a VRMMO addict like me knew little about. It was easy to find web pages like "recommended accessory brands, separated by age range," but making my decision based on that felt wrong.

"Hmmmm…"

I stretched and reached for the mug Yui was sitting on. The little pixie flitted off and landed instead on a flat-screen display that I wasn't using much anymore. I downed the rest of my lukewarm cappuccino.

Before this, I wasn't able to communicate with Yui in the real world without the AVIC (Audiovisual Interactive Communication) probe that I had built at school. But thanks to a wearable multi-device called the Augma that hit the market this April, that problem was a thing of the past. Based on the information coming from my visual sensor, Yui could map out the 3D objects on my desk, like cups and monitors, in real time and make herself appear in my view in a physically accurate manner, without clipping through objects or surfaces. She claimed she preferred the AVIC probe, because she could control its camera of her own volition, but that on its own wouldn't let me hear Yui's voice. I ought to be thankful to the Augma for making it possible to see my beloved little daughter in the real world at all.

It was with this thought in mind that I extended my hand,

letting Yui flap her tiny wings until she landed on my fingertip. I didn't feel any weight, of course, because she wasn't a physical object, but the warmth and texture of her pale-pink dress was so convincing that it was almost like I was seeing it in a virtual world. Now that she was much closer, I brushed Yui's head with my left hand and looked at the bed on the other side of my room.

Atop the blanket, which I'd aired out just earlier in the day, rested my headgear-type VR interface, the AmuSphere. After a year and a half of heavy use, its exterior was getting worn out, and the design that seemed so cool and fresh when I first saw it looked clunky next to the Augma—but I still preferred the full-dive experience over augmented reality or mixed reality.

"Say, Yui. I'm going to pick out Asuna's present on my own," I said, looking back at the fairy on my hand. "But before that, I can do a little research, right? I plan to buy it in person rather than ordering it, so I have a bit more time to work with."

Based solely on the nonverbal cue of the glance I gave toward the AmuSphere, the AI showed considerable perception in anticipating my intentions. Yui shrugged and said, "Well, I suppose I can't stop you. I'll be waiting for you in there!"

She jumped off my finger, bounced and rotated in the air, and then vanished into a little spray of light. I stood up from my chair and took the Augma off my left ear. The virtual desktop vanished at once, revealing a wider view of the room. In a moment, I turned to the west-facing window.

It was Sunday, September 27th. The fall equinox had passed just four days ago, but it already felt like the sunset was happening much earlier. It was only four o'clock, but the carpet of spotty cirrocumulus clouds above was already golden.

Much closer to the ground, flocks of birds were flying back to their nests for the night, and as I watched them, I thought I caught a glimpse of a white tower splitting the sunset in two.

The vision caused me to blink quickly several times.

I pressed a hand to my heart to shake off the sudden swell of emotion and then walked over to my bed. There, I put on the

AmuSphere and went to lie down with my head on a folded blanket.

Closing my eyes, I whispered the magic words:

"...Link Start."

And then rainbow light surrounded my mind, transporting me to a far-off fairyland.

2

As Kirito the spriggan swordsman, I set foot in the living room of a little log cabin in the forest of the twenty-second floor of New Aincrad, a floating castle that circled above the realm of Alfheim. A day in *ALO* was only sixteen hours long, but it just so happened to be late afternoon here as well, as golden sunlight was coming through the window.

Over time, our home had become a hangout spot for our friends, but at the moment, it was silent and empty. Asuna had said she was going to be out with her family until the evening, and Suguha hadn't come home from kendo practice yet. At least Yui should be waiting for me, I thought—but there was no sign of her in the darkened living room, either. Instead, all that awaited me was an incoming message icon blinking on the right side of my field of vision.

It was from the mace-wielding leprechaun warrior, Lisbeth.

As soon as I tapped the icon, a game window full of colorful emojis appeared.

Silica and I are raising our skill levels on the 45th floor. Come help us when you're done with homework! Oh, and we're borrowing Yui.

"......That would explain it."

At least I knew why my daughter wasn't around. In *ALO*, Yui was classified as a navigation pixie—an in-game helper with advanced player-assistance abilities. She could tell you what monsters would appear in an area and how fast they populated, which was very helpful when you were grinding. According to the game system, she was classified as my property, so before this, she only appeared if I was online and called her name, but lately she was showing up of her own accord as long as one of my friends was online. I was too afraid to ask her why.

But on the other hand, while Yui's capabilities were surely advanced enough that she could appear in two places at once—or ten, or a hundred—if she wanted, she refused to do such a thing. The tendency to fixate strongly on the singularity of their condition was a feature shared by all the AIs Akihiko Kayaba designed. Even the AR idol singer Yuna from the Ordinal Scale incident half a year earlier was no exception; she had nearly self-destructed because her agency had tried to copy her program.

"So what now…?" I murmured to myself, closing the message from Lisbeth.

I had dived into *ALO* so I could talk to her and Silica and do some sly research about what Asuna might like to receive as a present, but I couldn't bother them if they were busy playing. I thought about joining them for the fun of it, but the line in the message about "when you're done with homework" was a big mental disincentive. I still had a mini-report on a computer science experiment due tomorrow that wasn't finished yet.

I couldn't choose to ignore my homework, of course, but I was also falling behind in raising my skill levels in the game. Word was that a big new floor-boss battle was planned soon, and I wanted to get my combat senses honed again in time.

New Aincrad had been ported into *ALO* last May, with the first through tenth floors available to play. A September update had opened the tenth through twentieth floors, and in January, they'd made up to the thirtieth floor accessible. Regular updates had continued, making it possible to reach the fiftieth floor at the start of this month. You could tell that the development team, Ymir, was really putting their all into designing the bosses, because they'd gotten meaner and nastier with each update. As of today, September 27th, the farthest anyone had gotten was still only the forty-sixth floor.

Lisbeth was very excited about the chance to set up her own shop with a waterwheel in the town of Lindarth once the forty-eighth floor opened, like she had back in the original *SAO*. Agil had announced that he would have his own general store in Algade on the fiftieth floor, too. But at this pace, we wouldn't get to the former until next month—and near the end of the year for the latter. I wanted to make it up to them for helping me so much in the Underworld, and that meant I had to get my character stronger…

But it took all my willpower to pull back the foot that started to swing toward the door. There was no way a guy who was going to be eighteen years old in ten days should be ditching a school report to play games. I had the experiment data, so I could have everything wrapped up in an hour (I hoped). I sat at the virtual dining table and, from inside the game, accessed my home PC and called up the unfinished report and all the data related to it. Then, borrowing Asuna's magic mug—a quest reward that offered a random choice from among ninety-nine types of tea if you tapped it—I sipped on what smelled like mint-chocolate tea and began to type at the keyboard, telling myself "Okay! Let's shoot for finishing it in forty-five minutes!"

Throughout my life, even at my worst period of online game addiction, I never let my homework get backed up or overdue. The toughest part was during this summer vacation, because to the outside world, I had essentially been in a coma for an entire month.

I had been attacked and injected with succinylcholine by Johnny Black, a member of Aincrad's most infamous team of assassins, Laughing Coffin, and one of the architects of the Death Gun incident. The chemical put me into a state of cardiac arrest, right at the end of June, not long after vacation began. While I survived the ordeal, I didn't wake up again until August, and after a period of physical rehab, I was finally allowed to go back home on August 16th.

In other words, two-thirds of my forty-day summer vacation passed before I had time for myself, making a backlog of homework unavoidable. I probably could've asked for half of it to be forgiven, but to negotiate that, I'd have to explain to my school *why* I'd been in a coma.

They might believe that I was attacked on the street and hospitalized. But who would believe that I was abducted from the hospital in a fake ambulance, flown on a helicopter to a marine-research vessel in the distant southern seas, strapped to a mysterious machine that accessed the human soul, and sent into a strange place called the Underworld, where I cut down a giant cedar tree, went to a swordsmanship school, fought the ruler of the world, and entered a coma in *that* world, too...?

In the end, I had no choice but to get through it as best I could with the help of my friends. As I typed out my report, I thought back on that hellish final week of summer vacation and exorcised my frustration by grumbling aloud, "The least you could have done before you vanished was order them to release me from my homework obligations..."

No one was around to reply, of course. I was the only one in the forest cabin, and the man I was talking to hadn't shown up in Alfheim in ages.

The real-life player behind the undine mage Chrysheight was Seijirou Kikuoka, of the Ministry of Internal Affairs and Communications' Virtual Division. He had vanished from both the virtual world and the real world over a month ago.

Control of Kikuoka's shell company, Rath, was now in the hands of Dr. Rinko Koujiro, and as the chief technical officer, Takeru Higa was an even more vital figure than before. I had reason to hope for the future of the Underworld, bit by bit—but Kikuoka's disappearance left me with a strange feeling of loss.

If even I felt that way, after all the troubles and danger he put me through, I was sure the Rath staff were very subdued now. *He was a real pain in the ass, right to the end*, I thought…and then had to remind myself that he wasn't actually dead.

Kikuoka had passed himself off as a dead-end public servant in the ministry, but in fact, he was a lieutenant colonel in the Ground Self-Defense Force. He vanished from the Ground SDF at the same time as several senior officers of the Department of Defense, who were found to be allied with an American defense company responsible for attacking the *Ocean Turtle*. He probably wasn't in Japan at all at this point.

I didn't know if I would ever have the chance to see him again. But now that I was here in this second home of mine, far from the Underworld, even Kikuoka's stories about extremely stinky gourmet delicacies from all over the world were a fond memory.

Perhaps it was because I was indulging in uncharacteristic thoughts like these that I missed the sound of a character logging in. Only when the bouncing footsteps were right behind me did I notice them. I pushed the holo-window with my nearly complete report to the center of the table and turned around.

"I thought you were asleep, A—"

—suna.

I stopped myself before I could finish. The female avatar standing behind me was not the blue-haired undine I'd expected, but a feline cait sith, with triangular cat ears atop her head. Unlike other cait siths, she had none of their affectionate cuteness.

The hair that hung down to the middle of her back was dazzlingly golden. Her skin was so pale you could practically see through it. Her eyes were sapphire blue. All in all, her stunning beauty was very similar to her actual features…not in the real world, but in the Underworld.

"…H-hi, Alice. Good evening," I said, lifting my hand in greeting. The Integrity Knight Alice Synthesis Thirty just snorted, her ears twitching with displeasure.

"You seem rather disappointed that I'm not Asuna, Kirito."

"N-no, no, noooo! I'm not thinking that. At all!" I protested, shaking my head, but the knight's glare only grew colder.

I glanced down and realized that, despite the hour, she had golden armor and a golden longsword equipped over her blue dress.

"Oh...Are you going hunting?" I asked.

Rather than remove her scowl, Alice merely shifted it into a different permutation. "Yes, I had an agreement with Lisbeth. But...I will admit, I'm not used to this word *hunt*."

She pulled out the chair next to me and sat down with a clank. I rose to a standing position on instinct, then dashed off to the kitchen, telling her I'd put on some tea. When I came back, I had another magic tea mug and a tray featuring an unidentified pastry I'd found in the shared item storage.

I noticed Alice staring intently at my report window, which was still open over the table. When she noticed me coming, she looked up and asked, "Is this an assignment for the academy you attend?"

"Er...yeah, that's right."

"Hmm...When I was training at the cathedral, I was given piles of sacred arts assignments," she murmured. There was a faint smile on her lips, evoking a look of nostalgia and sadness.

I didn't know any human being who had experienced a fate as strange and checkered as Alice's.

She had been born in a tiny village in the distant northern reaches of the Underworld, where she'd lived until she was eleven, when she violated the Taboo Index's rule against trespassing into the Dark Territory and was summarily taken by an Integrity Knight to the Axiom Church's stronghold, Central Cathedral.

The all-powerful Administrator had performed the Synthesis Ritual upon her, causing Alice to lose all her memories. Eugeo and I made our way to the cathedral intent on taking her back, but she herself stood in our path as the strongest of the Integrity Knights. But when she learned of the Axiom Church's hypocrisy and the pontifex's cruelty, she broke through the seal that had blocked her mind's free thought and subsequently joined our side and helped defeat Administrator.

After that, she left the Church and settled into the forest outside Rulid, where, for half a year, she'd taken care of me while I was in a mentally comatose state, until word arrived that the ultimate war with the Dark Territory was beginning. She fought like a demon in the battle at the Eastern Gate but was ultimately abducted by the man who led the assault team on the *Ocean Turtle*. Thanks to the sacrifice made by Commander Bercouli, however, she was freed, and with Asuna's guidance, she logged out of the system console—and now she had a mechanical body developed by Takeru Higa that she used to live in the real world.

Whether she wanted to be or not, she was the world's first true general-purpose artificial intelligence. Her current schedule was very busy, assisting Dr. Koujiro with her mission to win human rights for AI, but it seemed she was able to log in to *ALO* frequently when she needed a break. Most likely, she found the fantasy world of Alfheim a lot more familiar than the sights of the real world.

"Yeah, I got plenty of assignments at Swordcraft Academy, too. I even remember the phrases for the sacred arts," I said, shrinking my homework window down to a corner of the table and setting down the mug and plate.

Alice's cat ears twitched. "Well, well. And what is the command to create a small hollow sphere of steel elements, filled with water, then warmed by heat elements from the outside?"

"*Hrrg!* W-well…the general rule is to generate elements from the most stable first, so I'd start with Generate Metallic…er, no, wait. The steel ball has to surround the water, so does the water element come first…?"

Alice suddenly made the most exhausted sigh I had ever heard, so I childishly retorted, "L-listen, it's fine. When you have my abilities, you don't need to say the words. Incarnation will do the trick instantly…"

"That's not the point!" she snapped, like a teacher. With complete familiarity, she tapped the rim of the mug and took a sip of the pale-pink tea that flooded up from the bottom. "Mmm…this is a good one."

Based on that reaction, she'd clearly been visiting regularly and having tea parties with Asuna—or something. *God help me*, I thought as I leaned back and tapped my own cup.

The tea that bubbled up was a deep reddish-purple; I tasted it with some foreboding, and the sourness that struck my tongue was like pickled plums ground up in a blender. I desperately snatched up the pastry and took a big bite, and thankfully, it was perfectly normal fruit pie. Alice approved as well, taking one bite and then another—with the fork, of course.

I cut through the sugar with another sip of mouth-puckering plum tea, then asked, "So…you were saying something about the word *hunt*?"

"Ah…yes, I was," Alice said with a nod. She turned her blue eyes to the darkness outside the window. "To me…and probably the rest of the human realm…hunting is the act of killing a wild animal for food, while thanking Terraria for her blessing. But the people of this world—these 'players'—kill unfathomable numbers of animals and monsters solely for the purpose of raising their authority level. I do not mean to say this is wicked. In the battle at the gate, I slaughtered hundreds, if not thousands, of demi-humans from the Dark Territory, after all. But…I do not wish to call it *hunting*."

"…I see," I said, nodding slowly.

Alice understood that Alfheim was a world created within the real world. But she was having trouble understanding the concept of a VRMMORPG…and what playing a "game" meant.

I couldn't blame her for that. In the sense that it was a virtual world, they were absolutely the same as her old home of the Underworld. Like the Underworld, Alfheim was just another place to her, and she could not share the conception among every other VRMMO player and me that these places were *temporary*.

So when I had first taken Alice from New Aincrad down to Alfheim, and we encountered a group of salamander PKers in the ancient forest near the sylph territory, it had turned into quite a scene. Silica took damage from a sneak attack, and Alice was so furious that she swore at the salamanders like some fierce demonic menace, until they were so intimidated that they apologized to Silica and left some money for her as recompense. I'd never even heard of such a thing happening.

Among the small group of players who knew that Alice the cat-eared knight of *ALO* was the artificial intelligence A.L.I.C.E. introduced at the splashy press conference last month, this incident became known as the Legend of Lady Alice Scolding the PKers Until They Cried. At any rate, I couldn't help but hope that the day would come when Alice learned to enjoy *ALO* for the game it was meant to be.

In the meantime, I'd finished my portion of the fruit pie and choked down about a third of my tea when I finally turned to the proud knight from another world and said, "I agree that the word *hunt* you hear in VRMMOs has drifted quite a distance from its original meaning. But the truth is, the vast majority of the population of modern Japan has no experience with real hunting—including me. When times and places change, so do words. I'm sure that phenomenon happened in the Underworld, too…"

"……"

Alice was initially silent because she was chewing the last bite of fruit pie, which she chased with the rest of her tea.

"Well, two hundred years have passed since I lived in the Underworld," she said, "so I suppose there has been a great change in not just language, but culture in general. Whatever change that might be, I must accept it…For one thing, the very existence of that change is proof that you protected and preserved the Underworld…"

Much to my consternation, Alice stared directly into my eyes and smiled. I did manage to mount a denial out of sheer habit, however. "But…it wasn't just me who did that. Asuna, Sugu, Sinon…in fact, there were *thousands* of players from *ALO* who went to the Underworld to protect it."

"Yes, that's right…In that sense, the use of one measly word seems a very insignificant thing," Alice said, looking back out the window. She was not seeing the coniferous forest, however, but the otherworld that existed far beyond it.

On the *Ocean Turtle*, which was still out at sea but shut down by the SDF, the Lightcube Cluster, which was the container for the Underworld, and its Main Visualizer were still active, but the situation was fluid, to say the least.

The anti-Rath conservative faction in the Department of Defense had temporarily lost power because of Kikuoka's sacrificial move, so for now, the Underworld was not going to be instantly scrapped. But that situation could change quickly based on how the struggle for control played out.

Early on the morning of August 18th, Asuna, Alice, and I had dived into the Underworld from Rath's office in Roppongi. We'd panicked briefly when we appeared out in space rather than on the ground, but with the help of the two young Integrity Knights—er, Integrity Pilots—whom we met flying their dragoncraft, we somehow made it back to the human realm.

But I was extremely conflicted about the idea of just marching into Central Cathedral. For one thing, whatever happened in the last two hundred years, Asuna and I were the Star King and Star Queen now and had apparently died thirty years ago. If we strolled through the front door and said "'Sup!" the entire cathedral, and probably the rest of the world with it, would go into an existential panic.

So the three of us allowed the pilot named Laurannei to guide us to her home in Centoria. The building was over four hundred years old, and it felt strangely familiar. There, the two pilots caught us up on the current state of the Underworld and even fed us a meal.

Before we dived, Dr. Koujiro told us she would wake us up by force once five hours had passed, so before we hit that point (fortunately, there were clocks in the Underworld now), we promised to meet the pilots again, and the three of us logged out.

I wanted to go back right away, to be honest, but Dr. Koujiro and Higa told us that we were forbidden to dive again until they had appraised the information we brought back from our trip, so they could assess the effects on the simulation.

I could understand why the adults were being careful. Whoever it was that told Alice the IP address she could use to connect to the Underworld—I had a vague idea—they were still unknown. And the direction the Underworld took in the times ahead would have a huge effect on the outcome of the plan to secure the Lightcube Cluster—and the issue of human rights for AI.

Fortunately, the Underworld was currently running in real time, not accelerated time. So there was nothing like before, where you might spend years inside the Underworld from a single login. Even still, a month had passed. Laurannei and Stica were probably feeling antsy, and I wanted to hear from *them* this time. For one thing, I was pretty sure they were actually—

"...rito. Kirito. Are you listening to me?"

The cat-eared knight jabbed my elbow, and I blinked back to the present. "Ah! Yes. Sorry, I was thinking about the Underworld..."

That caused Alice's face to soften out of scold mode. "I see. I find myself thinking about it several times a day."

"Yeah...I want to go back soon."

"Yes," she agreed, then sighed wistfully.

My longing for that place had to be nothing compared to the depth of Alice's homesickness. And she had two clear goals to achieve.

One was to re-hatch the eggs of her dragon, Amayori, and its brother, Takiguri—I'd rewound them into their pre-hatched forms before the final battle with Gabriel Miller.

The other was to awaken her sister, Selka Zuberg, who was in a deep freeze on the eightieth floor of Central Cathedral.

Neither would be easy—especially the latter. She would have to convince the current government of the human realm that she was none other than the legendary Integrity Knight Alice Synthesis Thirty, who had vanished over two hundred years before.

But I knew Alice could do it, and I would do anything I could to help, of course. I couldn't wait to see Selka again, either.

Before I could mentally travel to the Underworld yet again, Alice's voice pulled me back. "By the way, Kirito, I have a message from Dr. Koujiro."

"Uh...a message? Could she not just e-mail me?"

"Apparently, she did not want to leave traces on the network," she said.

I grimaced. The lines Rath used were safeguarded with very heavy security. If Dr. Koujiro wanted to avoid e-mail or even a spoken message, and instead relay her news through word of mouth in *ALO*, where there would be no record, it had to be very important information.

As I tensed, Alice announced, "The twenty-ninth, at fifteen o'clock. The expensive cake shop."

"......Huh?"

"That's all."

"......"

The twenty-ninth was two days from now. Fifteen o'clock was three in the afternoon. That part was clear.

But what was the "expensive cake shop"? There were plenty of places in Tokyo that fit that description. I bet I could even find one or two in Kawagoe City, Saitama Prefecture, where I lived.

I almost thought about sending Dr. Koujiro a message to double-check but stopped myself. If I made contact from this side, it would ruin the pains she'd taken to keep it secret.

As I mulled this over, rocking my head from side to side, Alice looked envious. "There are countless varieties of cake in the real world. So many things I never ate in Centoria. Looking at the pictures of them makes me hungry."

"Uh…yeah, I guess…But I really liked the sweets I used to buy in Centoria. Those honey pies? Three for just ten *shia*, and that filled a whole bag…"

"Are the cakes here expensive?"

"Well, I always imagined one *shia* being equivalent to about ten yen, so a nicer pastry shop might cost…oh, forty *shia* for one piece?"

"Th-that *does* sound expensive," she marveled, eyes wide.

I grinned. "And there's much fancier ones. I once had a piece of cake in Ginza that would be a hundred and sixty *shia*…"

But I stopped there, realizing something. Dr. Koujiro wasn't the kind of person who used such mockingly vague code words. Meaning this message about an "expensive cake shop" was literally just a message to her. She was relaying it from another person at Rath, and there was only one I could think of who would write this message.

My shoulders sagged, and I sighed. Alice looked at me with confusion. "What is it, Kirito?"

"Oh…it's fine. I figured out what the message means. Thanks for telling me, Alice."

"It was a very easy task…is what I would normally say…but…"

The golden knight's cat ears twitched as she thought, and a mischievous grin snuck onto her lips.

"Perhaps you can help me with my training, then," she said.

"Huh? Oh, boosting your skill proficiency…?"

There was only one reason that Alice the proud and regal knight had chosen to play as a cait sith, with their cat ears and cat tails: It was the easiest race for reaching the character class of dragoon, the knights who rode dragons.

But just because they were the easiest didn't mean it was actually easy. To ride a dragon, you needed very high skill levels in both taming and swords or spears. To improve at both at once, you needed to fight and fight, activating the triggers to increase proficiency in the weapon, while spending the skill points you earned on the Beast-Taming skill.

I thought it over, then returned the homework window I had pushed to the corner of the tabletop to its original size.

"Give me thirty minutes, then. Once I've finished this, we can go meet up with Liz and the gang and work on earning SP for—"

I was cut off by a light *swooshing* sound.

That was the noise of a player logging in. And there was only one other person who could appear directly in this log cabin…

I spun around in the chair at warp speed, and Alice followed by rotating smoothly, just as a slender avatar appeared before the doorway.

She had long, pale-blue hair, a battle dress that was mainly white, and a silver rapier at her side. Asuna the undine magician and fencer recognized Alice and me—and her expression steadily changed into one of surprise.

"W…welcome back, Asuna," I said, getting to my feet. At last, she smiled and lifted her hand to wave.

"Good evening, Kirito. Welcome, Alice."

"Pardon me for intruding, Asuna," replied Alice with the same smile. Perhaps it was just my imagination, but it felt like the temperature in the room had gone up a few degrees…

In any case, I still had to finish my homework. I cleared my throat and spoke again. "Um, I need to wrap up this report, so if you two don't mind, you can go ahead and meet with Liz—"

Before I could finish my sentence, there was a violent shaking that burst through the floor of the log cabin, and a low, deep roar like thunder drowned out all other noise.

"Eeeek!" the girls screamed. On pure instinct, I leaped, grabbing Alice with my right hand and Asuna with my left. Once I'd gotten them down in a crouch on the floor, there was another boom. The thick beams that crossed the ceiling creaked, and the mugs tumbled off the table.

There wouldn't be earthquakes in a virtual world, of course, and even if it *did* happen in Alfheim, it wouldn't do anything to New Aincrad, which was floating in the sky. Plus, if New Aincrad were to somehow shake, it wouldn't mean the cabin's collapse.

But even though the logical part of my brain knew all this, my instincts kicked in, and I shouted, "Get outside, you two!"

I rushed across the roiling floor, practically dragging the fencer and cat-eared knight, and made it to the doorway. As soon as I pushed it open and leaped out onto the porch, the third and largest shock hit my legs, and the three of us tumbled down the porch steps.

Fortunately, the front yard was just grass, so we didn't lose any HP. I was about to unfold my fairy wings, thinking that at least if I was floating, the shaking ground would stop affecting me—when Asuna grabbed my hand with all her strength.

"Kirito, l-look…!" she gasped.

Her trembling hand was pointing at the blue sky visible through the outer aperture, which was very close by. A second later, I noticed it, too.

Alfheim's internal time was not synced to the real world, so it was still afternoon, far from sundown, but the horizon was blazing red now. The bloodred color was coming this way at astounding speed and soon covered New Aincrad's entire sky.

"…That is not a sunset…," said Alice, who was clutching my other hand. Hardly any of the words were penetrating my consciousness, but I was screaming the same thing inside my mind anyway.

It wasn't just that the horizon was red—a hexagonal pattern was rapidly filling the sky. On the hexagons was an alternating array of the words *Warning* and *System Announcement*.

"Kirito," Asuna called again, her voice frail.

I squeezed her delicate hand, but my mind was vividly replaying memories of the last time I saw a sky like this: a very fateful day, indeed.

It was nearly four years ago, on November 6th, 2022.

At five thirty PM on the day of the launch of the world's first VRMMORPG, *Sword Art Online*, ten thousand players were automatically teleported to the square of the Town of Beginnings, where a pattern of crimson hexagons began to fill the sky.

The titanic game master appeared by dripping downward from that sky and, in a deep and menacing voice, announced, *Welcome to my world, dear players.* From that moment on, Asuna and I and nearly ten thousand others were trapped in a deadly game with no ability to log out. It'd taken two whole years of real time for us to finally escape.

Is that going to happen all over again?

No. It wasn't possible. Asuna and I were wearing AmuSpheres, which had many layers of security and safety measures, not the old NerveGear, and Alice did not require an interface machine to log in to *ALO*. Even if the LOG OUT button on the menu was gone, we would be fine as soon as someone in the real world pulled the AmuSpheres off our heads.

So what did this red sky represent, then?

Some surprise in-game event? That was hard to imagine. There was no way, in terms of compliance, that they'd mimic the very event in *SAO* that led to four thousand deaths—no matter that Ymir, the company that ran *ALO*, was a small venture-funded firm.

Was the server hacked from the outside? It wasn't impossible, but while it was probably easy to overwrite the skybox texture, actually shaking all of New Aincrad like that had to be impossibly difficult. There was no magic or item that could produce that kind of effect in this world.

But no sooner had that thought entered my mind than a fourth shock hit us.

The ground of the twenty-second floor rippled like liquid, and cracks appeared in the green grass. The log cabin behind us screamed and creaked, and Asuna clutched the railing of the porch with both hands.

"Asuna!" I shouted—but then I figured it out. The blue-haired undine wasn't trying to keep herself upright; she was trying to prevent the house from collapsing. I rushed over instantly and pushed against the wall. Alice did her part by pressing on top of the porch to keep it in place.

But of course, the three of us alone could not outdo the destructive shaking. A hundred players would have no more luck than us. The entire six-mile length of the floating castle's floor was rumbling beneath us.

"Ah…!" Asuna shrieked as a dry bursting sound drowned her out. The triangular roof over the cabin's porch split in two. If the shaking persisted, the entire house would suffer similar damage in less than a minute.

I had a powerful attachment to this cabin, too, if not quite on the level of Asuna. The log cabin we had lived in as newlyweds for two happy weeks in the original Aincrad was destroyed when the deadly game was finished, but this one, which had appeared in New Aincrad when it was introduced to *ALO* half a year later, was copied straight from the *SAO* server. It was the real thing. Every detail about it was the same, from the patterns in the floorboards to the knots on the load-bearing beams.

In fact, even the Aincrad from the old *SAO* server was secretly recovered by Akihiko Kayaba's old teacher, Professor Tamotsu Shigemura…but at this point, that server was something of a grave marker for the professor's only daughter, Yuna, who had saved many lives in the Ordinal Scale incident this past April. It was deep in the fifth basement level of the off-limits Argus building, so it wouldn't be easy to access—nor did I want to. At this point, the cabin here was the place Asuna and I called home to our many memories together.

With that thought fueling me, I dug my fingers into the log wall and used all my strength to try to hold it still.

Then the vibrations stopped, as though they had never happened at all.

In the moment, I felt relief that the shaking was over at last—but then I noticed that while the fiercest rumbling was gone, the ground itself was slowly tilted forward…leaning us toward the outer edge of the floating castle.

"What's this…?!"

Gripped by an unprecedented sense of foreboding, I spun around.

And then I was rendered speechless.

Just five to ten feet away from the fence line that marked the edge of the cabin's plot, the ground ended.

The shaking had split the very floor of New Aincrad itself. The ground we were standing on now was floating in the air—no, falling. *That* was why the shaking stopped.

A moment later, Asuna and Alice came to the same realization and found their voices.

"Kirito...the ground!"

"The house is falling, Kirito!"

I was aware of that, but I had no idea what to do about it. I could only watch in disbelief as the slice of the twenty-second floor drifted away. Perhaps our falling speed seemed slow because the chunk of the floor carrying the log cabin was over a hundred yards across and was suffering from major air resistance. If we were in a total free fall, our feet would be pulling away from the ground, but I could still walk, if with a reduced sense of gravity.

A part of me was optimistic enough to hope that the house might not be destroyed when we landed, but I stifled that feeling at once. New Aincrad was floating thirty thousand feet above Alfheim. Even with the virtual air acting as a brake, the little island we were located upon was going to be smashed to atoms after a fall of that height, leaving nothing but a crater behind. Maybe the land itself would be fine, since VR terrain was considered indestructible—but our HP and the cabin's durability would be blasted to nothingness instantly.

No, wait...

Asuna, Alice, and I could survive. We had fairy wings, after all, so we could escape that grisly end by simply spreading them and flying. But I didn't think Asuna would choose that method. She knew that we were falling, but she still clung white-knuckled to the railing of the porch and wasn't going to let go now.

I watched the floating castle drift farther away from us, my hand similarly pressed to the wall of the cabin.

It seemed the entire castle itself was falling, not just these isolated islands of earth. I didn't know what happened to New Aincrad, but there was no doubting this was an unprecedented catastrophe in motion. Beneath the reddened sky, the massive conical silhouette tilted in a southern direction and continued to fall. Islands of rock about the size of what we were resting upon broke off from the floors below us.

Lisbeth, Silica, and Yui were leveling up on the forty-fifth floor of New Aincrad, if I recalled. I was worried about them, but the most important thing right now was to find a way to save this log cabin. If a person falling from a height of thirty thousand feet spread out their limbs to maximize air resistance, it would take about three minutes for them to reach the ground, according to something I felt like I'd read before. That meant we probably had about the same time until this little island made contact with Alfheim on the ground. But because this was the virtual world, it could be faster or slower.

To cut through the roaring of the air around us, I screamed at the top of my lungs, "Dammit! If this were the Underworld, I could use my Incarnate power to lift this stupid rock right up!"

Immediately, the cat-eared knight clinging to the porch snapped back, "Stop trying to use Incarnation to solve every problem you have!"

"I-if there's any situation that calls for it, this would be it!"

"It is during the greatest emergencies that a knight's mindset is tested the most!"

Asuna had recovered some of her wits, and she cut into our squabbling firmly: "You might not be able to use Incarnation, but there might still be something we can do!"

The way she said that made me think for an instant that Asuna might actually be able to call upon Stacia's geography-shaping powers here in this world, too. But of course, her answer was something completely different.

"Let's use our wings to push this rock!"

"What…?! You know there's no way for us to lift a chunk of earth this big—," I protested, but Asuna shook her head.

"No, we're not going to lift it, just change the trajectory. If we can push it to land in the right spot, then maybe…"

"Oh…I—I get it!" I exclaimed, reading the intention of my longtime partner. "If we drop it onto water, or maybe sand or swamp, the shock should be alleviated somewhat!"

"I see," murmured Alice, nodding. She spread her fairy wings. Asuna and I pulled away from the cabin and jumped. Since we were free-falling, it took only a little upward lift for our avatars to rise quickly off the ground.

At a hundred yards above the roof of the cabin, we stopped buzzing our wings and maintained distance as we resumed falling. In a (relative) hover over the little island, it was clear that the chunk of land was like a piece of shortcake, a hundred yards at most on one side, but two hundred on the other. The cabin was on the narrower end, so if we could drop the wider end into the water first, perhaps there was a chance our home could be saved—or so I wanted to believe.

I looked beyond the island. The land far in the distance below was a brilliant-green forest. Only in the sylph and undine territories was there such a large, lush forest, but the shining reflection of water here and there meant that, of the two, it had to be undine land.

That was lucky for us. The force the three of us could create together was minuscule, but with that many lakes below, there was less distance we might need to push to get it to land in one of them—or so I hoped.

With great concentration, I focused on the diagonal descending trajectory of the falling island. I could see several lakes below, but none of them seemed like the right match in terms of size and shape. The ideal body of water would be long and narrow, like an airport runway, but that was too convenient to hope for—

"Oh…there!"

"That way!" Asuna and I shouted together. The glittering surface in the far distance was probably a river, not a lake, but it was plenty wide enough to give the island a soft, watery landing. It was located along the trajectory of the island's fall, too. Just a shift of two hundred yards to the right should do the trick.

"Let's hurry!"

Alice spread her wings again. The three of us shot into a descent toward the left side of the island. As soon as I passed over the edge of the plummeting rock, a huge increase in air resistance pushed me back upward, but I did my best to dive and cut through it until I was down at the side of the rock layer.

Our elevation at this point was about four thousand yards. So for every twenty yards we fell, one yard of lateral movement should put us safely into the river. The three of us could never move an entire chunk of land like this while resting on the surface. It was only possible while airborne.

I pressed my hands against the dark rock side and shook my wings as hard as I could.

"Rrrraaaaah!"

On my right, Asuna joined in, with Alice on the left.

"Urrrrhhh!!"

"Upsy-daisy!!"

That struck me as an odd thing for a regal Integrity Knight and young woman to say, but now wasn't the time for critique.

If we had tried this during the period when RCT Progress managed *ALO*, our flight gauge would have dried up in moments, leaving us helpless to fall. But the new management team, Ymir, was much more generous and eliminated all limitations on flight. We could use all the energy we wanted without running out. The hunk of rock, four hundred yards at its longest, resisted our efforts initially like the goliath it was, but as we persisted, its path slowly budged.

"If we push it too far, we won't be able to course correct!" Alice warned. We could only follow our instincts at this point.

"But even now, us getting it there is a long shot…I think! Don't be timid—just push!"

"I'm trusting in your good luck, Kirito!" Asuna shouted. Well, I had no trust in that luck. I just had to tell myself that if I'd been saving it up, this was the moment to use it.

For over ten seconds, we strained and pushed the island through the howling wind.

The ground was much closer now. We were only a thousand yards up…nine hundred…eight hundred. I couldn't see the river yet, looking down past the side of the rock. Without realizing it, I started to kick my legs in a subconscious attempt to add force. My every ounce of strength was dedicated to pushing.

Then there was light shining below. A water surface…

"That's the river! Push for five more seconds, then disengage!" I shouted. Asuna promptly began a countdown.

"Four! Three! Two! One! Now!"

The three of us spread our wings to go into a sudden stop. I felt it jolting my body backward, and I nearly went into a tailspin, but we locked our arms to stay stable and upright.

The huge shortcake-shaped piece of rock hurtled downward toward the water, rear end first. The log cabin still clung to the pointed end, ceiling slats and fence posts flying loose, but the building stubbornly refused to collapse.

As long as the water absorbed enough of the impact…

I prayed to a god that probably wasn't present in this virtual world as the moment of fate approached.

Three seconds later, the base of the chunk of rock made contact with the surface of the water.

A curtain of blue burst high into the air on the far end. Moving water was an area in virtual reality that had a tendency to be abbreviated to save processing power, but the realism of the jet of water here amazed me; I couldn't believe *ALO* was able to depict such details. The island bounced, then bounced again, and again. With each impact, the cabin creaked and cracked.

Please hang in there! I pleaded, but as if to mock me, the island of rock split down the middle. The water pushed back harder this time, and the little island, nearly vertical at this point, was unable to withstand the kinetic energy involved and broke over the middle.

"Aaah…!" Asuna wailed. I clutched her trembling hand.

The tip of the little island containing our log cabin broke off of the rear wedge and flew through the air. Up ahead, the river curved sharply, so there wasn't much water left in that direction to cushion the impact. Beyond the river was thick forest. The piece of rock plunged into it, sending huge conifer trees into the air. A choking cloud of dirt and dust billowed upward, blocking our sight.

Lastly, there was a deep rumbling…and then it was bizarrely silent.

I was trapped between the desire to see what happened to the log cabin and an aversion to seeing it completely shattered into pieces. Neither Asuna nor Alice said a word. We just hovered there, all three of us, watching the trail of rising dust.

Oh, but what about the rest of New Aincrad? That was falling along with us.

I was just turning around to survey the fate of the floating castle—when two things happened in succession.

First, the pattern of hexagonal red warning messages that filled the sky dissipated toward the horizon at the same speed with which it arrived.

Then the power that was keeping my body aloft vanished.

"Wha—?!" I yelped, trying to vibrate the wings on my back, but it did not create the tiniest piconeutron of upward force. The girls screamed, and we all began to plummet headfirst toward the surface of the river, three hundred feet below.

I thought something was wrong with my voluntary flight mechanism, so I waved my left hand to bring out the assistance controller. Yet my fingers closed on nothing but thin air. And I didn't stop falling. A fall from this height, even into water, was going to cause catastrophic damage.

Then it occurred to me that, if the three of us died, our respawn point was set to the log cabin. If the log cabin was destroyed or gone, where would we start over? The nearest town? The previous spawn point before that, in Yggdrasil City?

And if our log cabin was gone, it still contained all the items we were storing within it, including some things with memories attached to them. We'd need to get them back. If we resurrected somewhere very far away, could we get back here before all those items rotted away? We had to avoid dying here.

"Curl up into a ball, you two!"

In *ALO*—as in *SAO*, in fact—falling damage was affected by your position when you landed. If there was ground below, you wanted to land on your feet, but if there was water of indeterminate depth, a totally defensive position was safest. Press your legs up to your chest, put your arms over your head, and hold your breath.

Impact. My HP immediately halved.

Something in my mind raised a question when it happened. But I didn't have the wherewithal to pursue the source of that question now. Frothy bubbles burst from my mouth, and blue water flooded into me as I sank. I stretched out my limbs, trying to stop the descent, struggling toward the surface.

"*Bwaaah!!*"

I gasped for air when my head breached the surface of the river. Shortly after, Asuna and Alice rose as well. They seemed to have suffered the same amount of damage I did.

But it wasn't smart to tread water with your HP half gone. I didn't know much about undine territory, but big rivers like this one usually harbored alligators and turtles and eels and monsters of the like. Better that we get to the riverbank before they started to nibble on our toes.

"...We really can't fly anymore...," Alice mumbled. I saw that her wings were simply gone. And strangely, although Alice's cat ears were still there, Asuna's longer elfish ears looked human again. My ears probably were, too. My sense of foreboding rose, but safety was the top priority now.

"We'll just have to swim," I said. The other two nodded. There wasn't much else to do but swim toward the right bank, in the direction the log cabin fell.

Fortunately, no predators leaped out of the water at us. We reached solid ground, soaking wet, and paused to catch our breath. Asuna's gasping seemed like more than just exhaustion, so I reached out to steady her.

In the forest ahead, the trees had been knocked down as violently as though the giant beasts of Jotunheim had charged through them. The dust-cloud effects had subsided, but the little island carrying the log cabin was out of sight from here. Either it was hidden by the undulations of the land—or it had simply been obliterated.

"...I'm all right," Asuna whispered, straightening up. "We need to find out what happened to our home."

"I'm sure it's fine," said Alice as she approached, shaking off excess water. She reached up to brush one of her triangular ears and noted, "It's not drying off..."

Indeed, water was still dripping from the sleeves and hem of my black coat. The current version of *ALO* sold itself on ease of play, so the extremely unpleasant "wetness effect" didn't normally last. Within seconds of leaving the water, your hair and clothes were supposed to be perfectly dry again.

Maybe the fall of New Aincrad wasn't just some freakish occurrence, but only a part of some greater and more serious disruption. Struck with more foreboding, I waved my hand to call up my menu and ensure my weapons were equipped.

But the menu did not appear.

"Oh, you've gotta be kidding me..."

I made a flicking motion with two fingers, back and forth. But the usual sound effect would not accompany any of my movements. I tried it with my right hand and had no more success.

We're not really doing this *again, are we...?* I thought, feeling a shiver down my back.

But then there was a faint jingling sound, and a little window appeared below my raised right hand. I hastily examined it and saw a very plain font reading *Tips: To call up the menu window, make a clockwise circle with the index and middle fingers of your right hand.*

"...A circle?"

I was nonplussed but did as advised, drawing a circle in the air with two fingers, about four inches across.

With a strange, different sound, a faintly purple menu window appeared. I was momentarily relieved—until I saw the contents of the window, and along with Asuna and Alice, I gasped.

For one thing, the menu screen was not the familiar square layout from *SAO* and *ALO*, but a circle of simple icons—a ring menu. That wasn't a particularly rare format, but I hadn't heard anything about *ALO* changing up its UI.

Stunned, I moved my fingers around the window. Each icon they momentarily hovered over grew larger and displayed an English alphabet overlay. Going clockwise from the top, the icons were for STATUS, SKILLS, EQUIPMENT, STORAGE, QUESTS, MAP, COMMUNICATION, and SYSTEM. A very orthodox menu set for an MMORPG, but even that felt cold and strange under the circumstances.

I flicked the SYSTEM icon in the upper left with stiff fingers. Circular icons rotated and multiplied, displaying a number of submenus. Graphics, sound, UI settings—and a door-shaped icon for logging out.

"Whew...," Asuna and I said in unison, sighing. Alice was a bit puzzled at first but then realized why we were relieved.

"Ah, you were thinking of *Sword Art Online*."

"That's right...," said Asuna with a grim smile. "The Amu-Sphere was designed with safety in mind, so the same thing can't possibly happen again...but whenever anything out of the expected happens in a virtual world, I can't help but get jumpy."

"That seems like a natural reaction," said the knight with a rare expression of warmth—mean as that might be to say about her. But then she shook her head and returned to her usual brisk tone. "I cannot understand that Kayaba man, however. Over a hundred thousand humans die every day in the real world, so why would he lock young people within this supposedly safe virtual world and force them to risk death and fight against monsters and other human beings...? What would he get out of that?"

Neither Asuna nor I could answer this extremely direct question. What did—what *does* Akihiko Kayaba want? We'd been thinking about this for nearly four years and come no closer to understanding his motivations.

"...If you want to know, I think you'd have to ask him directly. Though, I doubt he'd give you a straight answer," I said, dismissing the SYSTEM icon. For sheer safety reasons, we should probably log out first, but before that, I wanted to check the log cabin's status.

But actually, there was another thing to determine first. What happened to the rest of New Aincrad, which should have fallen to earth a little bit later than the cabin? I couldn't imagine such a massive construct simply shattering without a trace. Any players who were stuck inside might have taken fall damage after plummeting from such a great height.

I wanted to send a message to Lisbeth, who'd gone to the forty-fifth floor to level-up her skills with Silica, so I reached for the COMMUNICATION icon but stopped myself. There was a quicker way to do this than tapping away at a holo-keyboard.

"Yui, are you there?" I said into thin air, and then I waited. Asuna and Alice looked at the air, too.

Yui, the artificial intelligence born in *SAO*, was registered in the *ALO* system as my personal navigation pixie. Unlike other pixies, she could act on her own elsewhere, but if I called her name, she could appear instantly in my presence, no matter where on the world map she was.

Under normal circumstances, that is.

"......"

I waited and waited, but nothing happened. Every other time I did this, she immediately popped into being in the air nearby.

"...Kirito, what happened to Yui?" Asuna mumbled in concern.

I tried to contain my rising panic. "She was with Liz's group on the forty-fifth floor, I'm pretty sure..."

"Then she should be connected to *ALO*," Asuna said. I hesitated but was about to agree with that statement, when Alice stepped forward and looked up at the sky, now blue again.

"I suppose the question is...are we even in Alfheim anymore?"

"Huh...? Wh-what do you mean?" I stammered.

Alice turned her blue eyes toward the forest behind us. "Though you may not have been aware of it, Kirito, the variety of plant life in Alfheim was very limited compared to the Underworld—and especially to the real world. There were only thirty or so varieties of trees, between deciduous and coniferous...But there are many kinds of trees in that forest that I have never seen in Alfheim."

"Oh...Now that you mention it...," murmured Asuna. I joined her in staring at the green of the forest. The detail on the terrain seemed very high...but I couldn't tell the kinds of trees apart. Asuna had an interest in rare trees and wooden furniture, however, and she seemed to agree with the assessment.

She turned to me and said, "Alice is right. There are all kinds of trees here that didn't grow in Alfheim. Plus...I thought something else was strange."

"Strange? How?"

"There are many lakes in Alfheim's undine territory, but they're mostly connected through underground reservoirs. There are no major rivers there like this one."

Now that she pointed it out, it seemed accurate to me, but I knew that thirty minutes ago, I dived into *ALO* from my device, and there were no terrain maps in *ALO* aside from Alfheim itself. Perhaps the other realms of Norse mythology like Asgard, realm of the Aesir, or Vanaheim, home of the Vanir, had been added as a surprise event. But this seemed too violent and chaotic to be something like that.

"…But we're definitely still in *ALO*, and that means Yui should respond to a summons," I said, as though trying to convince myself. I reached for the ring menu again and deployed the STATUS icon at the top of the circle. The round icon swished and expanded, splitting into four parts and giving way to a rectangular window.

"See, here's all my character data, just where I…"

My words vanished like smoke.

Right at the top of the window was my avatar name: *Kirito*.

But that was the only part of my character status that I recognized.

To the right of my name was a shining bit of text that said *Lv. 1*. Below it, four colored bars. In order, they were for HP, MP, TP, and SP. Above the HP bar, it said *98/200*, while the MP, TP, and SP bars all glowed white and said *100/100*.

HP and MP were pretty obvious—but what about TP and SP? And even worse…

"……Level-1……"

Asuna and Alice heard me groan and stared at me, then made the same circle with their hands in the air to open the ring menu. Once they could see their status windows, they reported in together.

"It says I'm level-1, too!"

"So am I!"

"What's going on?!"

"What is the meaning of this?!"

They turned toward me, but all I could do was shake my head, quivering. "I—I don't know why you're asking me…I'm ultra-shocked, myself…But the thing is, *ALO* isn't supposed…"

…to have levels. I could hear Agil's voice replaying what he said

when he was teaching me about how this game worked, a year and a half ago.

It's heavily skill-focused, meaning there's no level system. You just improve your skills through usage, and for the most part, your hit points don't go up at all.

For some reason, I also got a vivid mental image of the bald shopkeeper flashing me a smile and a thumbs-up. Annoyed, I banished the image so I could think this over.

If not just the UI had been changed, but even the level/skill system that was the root of the player's progression, then this was beyond the bounds of a mere update. It was clear this was no longer the *ALfheim Online* I knew.

I looked away from the level-1 character data and examined the bar gauges in the upper left of my vision. My HP bar had barely budged from its halfway point after falling into the river. Below that was a green MP bar and two more new bars below it. The blue one was presumably TP, and the yellow was SP. The reason I felt weird when I saw my HP bar while falling was probably my subconscious noticing that there were extra, unfamiliar elements in the display.

"...I think the moment our wings vanished, and we fell...that was when the system switched over...And our ears changed...," I murmured.

Asuna brushed her shortened ears and added, "This can't be a normal update if they completely reset our character data. And the UI is too polished for this to be some kind of accident or bug..."

"That's true," I said, circling the menu with my finger. The way the icons expanded and contracted was very smooth, and they had clearly been painstakingly programmed.

I didn't see a notification icon for received messages, but I thought that perhaps there was a notice to players from Ymir, the development team, so I selected the COMMUNICATION icon. It displayed sub-icons for PARTY, FRIENDS, and MESSAGES. I picked the third one.

There wasn't a single new message in the window that appeared. In fact, the entire contents of the inbox were gone. On top of that, my friends list was empty. Now I couldn't send messages to Liz and Silica's group.

"So both our stats and our friends list have been completely wiped," I said with a sigh.

Alice shook her head, blond hair swaying. "But we haven't lost everything, have we? We still have these."

She lifted her left hand and tapped the golden gauntlet still equipped on it. Indeed, both Asuna and I still had our armor on. Our gear had been crafted for us by Lisbeth with carefully assembled materials, or earned by running difficult dungeons in New Aincrad, so if anything was going to be left behind, at least it was our gear. And the water it had absorbed was finally drying out.

If our armor was still here, then the weapons we didn't have equipped should be, too, I hoped…and checked the item storage menu.

The item list had also been given a face-lift from its old simple text format. Now there were square graphical icons for each item arranged in a grid, so you could see how they looked without taking them out. It was easier to view, certainly, but the problem was that my enormous grid contained only two little icons.

Both of them were one-handed swords. One was Blárkveld, a piece made by Lisbeth's armory, and the other was the holy sword Excalibur, which I'd earned in Jotunheim. All the other items that had packed my inventory previously were gone without a trace.

"I only have my swords…," I groaned.

Meanwhile, Asuna and Alice looked up from their own screens to chime in.

"Me too. I only have my rapier and staff."

"The same goes for me. I have my sword and shield."

"Hmm…I know I had other weapons in there, too. Why are only my favorite ones left…?" I wondered.

Alice shrugged. "Perhaps it's because they're your favorites?

The items with the longest period of usage were left, and all the others vanished…"

"I see. In that case…this must be a man-made phenomenon. No bug or accident would conveniently leave you with your favorite gear."

To bring it out of my inventory, I tapped the icon of my usual sword, Blárkveld, and selected equip from the submenu. The sword's icon vanished, and I felt a comfortingly familiar weight on my back—

"Bwauh…?!"

But in fact, the weight went far beyond comforting. It felt like I had a gigantic steel construction bar roped to my back. My knees buckled, and to avoid falling clumsily on my butt, I swung my arms out and instinctually grasped whatever my fingers could squeeze.

"Eeeek!"

"Hey, what are you—?!"

The two screams caused me to look up, and I saw that my right hand was holding Asuna's sword belt, while my left hand was holding Alice's. It was the least gentlemanly thing I could do, but if I let go, all was lost. I would fall right onto the gravel of the riverbank.

"S-sorry, just hang on a bit longer!" I pleaded as they continued to shriek. At last, I barely managed to pull myself up to the point that I could touch the ground with one knee, rather than my bottom. I let go of the ladies' sword belts and put my hands on the ground where they could support my upper body.

I'd narrowly avoided toppling over, but the weight of the sword was still intense. I could not stand up. In the space to the right of my HP bar, there was a metal paperweight icon blinking red. I'd never seen it before, but the meaning was clear: I was over my encumbrance limit. But why?

The answer to that question came from Asuna, her face red as she pulled up on her belt.

"Oh, I see…Because all our stats were reset, the amount of

weight we can equip went down. That's the latest sword Liz made for you, right? Of course you can't lift it with starter stats."

"Ugh, are you serious…? So they left it with me, but I can't even use it…?" I grumbled, checking the status screen that I still had open. There were two meters that appeared to be related to encumbrance. The one on top said *Equip Weight*, while the one on bottom said *Carry Weight*. That was fairly straightforward. The Carry Weight meter, which presumably corresponded to my inventory as a whole, was only a third full, but the Equip Weight meter was bright red and completely full to the right edge. In that sense, having the carry weight be almost a third full just from a single weapon in storage—legendary Excalibur or not—was rather troubling.

"Yikes…if we don't have any usable weapons, we're not going to stand a chance if any monsters attack us right now," I pointed out.

Asuna nodded, her expression grim. "That's true. And I'm guessing our magic skills have been reset…too……"

She trailed off unnaturally, so I looked away from the status screen. Her face was slack, staring into space like her soul had left her body. Then she snapped back to attention and spun the ring menu with incredible speed. Based on the way her fingers moved, I guessed it was the skill menu she was opening and examining.

"Wh-what's up, Asuna?"

The undine did not answer. She just tapped a part of the window with a trembling finger, then a few seconds later, she exhaled with supreme relief.

"…What's up?" I asked again, still down on my knee.

Asuna looked at me and smiled weakly. "I thought we might have lost our weapon skills…and all the sword skills we learned, too. But…while magic and medicinal mixing skills might be gone, I still have the Rapier skill. My proficiency and sword skills are still there."

That was when I understood at last. There was another thing

here that Asuna treasured at least as much as that log cabin. It was the original sword skill, Mother's Rosario, which had been given to her by Yuuki, the ultimate warrior, who had passed into eternal sleep just half a year ago. Fortunately, that and all the other techniques she'd learned were still here.

"Mm-hmm...I have my One-Handed Sword skill, too. Like with the weapons, it would seem that the skill with the highest proficiency has been retained," said Alice. She was probably correct about that. That meant my One-Handed Sword skill was safe, too.

I turned to Asuna and wondered, "Um...so, Asuna, does that mean your Rapier skill was higher than your Water Magic skill...?"

"Is there a problem with that?" she asked, glaring.

I hastily shook my head. "N-no, none at all. I was just thinking about that Berserk Healer title of yours..."

"Now that I don't have any magic skills, I relinquish that title," Asuna said, turning her head aside in a huff. When she looked back, she added, "And how long are you going to keep doing that, Kirito? There's no point to carrying around a sword you can't hold. Put it back in your inventory."

"F-fine, fine..."

But in one last attempt at resistance, I tried to get to my feet with Blárkveld on my back. The only thing that happened was a trembling in my knees—and no lift. I groaned and strained but produced nothing other than a pair of sighs from Asuna and Alice.

My effort wasn't fruitless, however.

There was a swishing, jingling sound effect, and a little window appeared before my eyes. I blinked repeatedly as I read the message: *Physique skill gained. Proficiency has risen to 1.*

So this world seemed to share the same skill-based system as *ALO*. When the player's actions fulfilled the proficiency trigger conditions, it would roll for the chance to acquire a skill or increase its proficiency level. I'd never seen this Physique skill before, but it was probably similar to the Carry Limit Expansion from *SAO*, so the higher my proficiency got, the heavier weight I could carry.

In other words, if I kept bearing the incredible weight of my sword, it would steadily increase my Physique skill to the point that the red over-encumbered icon would disappear—but I didn't know how many hours or even days that would take. It was better to obey Asuna's command and go back to my equipment screen, then drag the BLÁRKVELD icon in my right-hand space over to the inventory area and drop it.

Instantly, the weight on my back vanished, and I sprang to my feet. I stretched, loosened my cramped muscles—all just a mental illusion, of course—and looked toward the direction the log cabin fell. The girls silently gazed over the river with me.

"...Let's go," I murmured, and they nodded. I was nervous about walking into the forest without a weapon equipped, but we couldn't just sit here on the riverbank and wait forever.

The riverbank was littered with large and small stones. I had a sudden thought, so I went into the ring menu and selected COMMUNICATION, then PARTY, and finally tapped the INVITE icon so I could throw invitations to Asuna and Alice. When they accepted, new gauges appeared in the upper left of my field of view. That basic interface functionality was the same as *ALO*, *GGO*, and *SAO*, so I could guess that we were in a VRMMO world based on the Seed engine, at the very least.

"HP and MP I understand, but what are these TP and SP bars for...?" Asuna asked as we walked. They were both full and not changing, so there was no way to tell for now.

"I suppose it will be clear when they go down," said Alice, who was on the same train of thought.

Asuna grinned and said, "I guess you're right."

These two might get along better than they realize, I thought but didn't dare say aloud.

Eventually, our careful hike through the rocks got us to the front end of the terrible gouge where the cabin fell into the forest. Massive trees were torn up from the roots, which was shocking to see, but at least they offered a bit of a blockade against any monsters that might be around.

Before we stepped into the fresh scars upon the earth, I checked my MAP icon just to be sure, but as I suspected, it only contained the mapped areas we'd seen for ourselves. Whether this was indeed the undine territory of Alfheim or not, the map data had been reset. But at least I could tell that we were walking in a northeast direction—assuming "up" on the map meant north.

We made our way carefully through the disordered labyrinth of felled tree trunks, climbing over, ducking under, and squeezing through the empty spaces, until after about fifty feet, we found our way blocked by a wall of lumber as tall as our avatars. It would be a simple hop over it if we still had our wings, but this time we had no choice but to climb.

"Here we go…"

This was reminding me of being a kid and playing with my sister, Suguha, on the adventure park obstacle course at Isanuma Park, in my hometown of Kawagoe.

I was halfway up the wall when Asuna said, "Ah…what if we…?" and tapped the log my right foot was resting on. A window rotated into existence with a little swishing sound effect.

"Aha, I was right! This log is treated as a material item. I think it'll go into our inventory if we select it."

"W-wait, not until I'm done climbing off of—," I said, when suddenly the huge log under my foot glowed blue and disappeared. "*Nwaaa!!*"

My leg split empty air. With nothing to support me, I *did* fall properly on my butt this time, and then a number of other tree trunks rolled toward me without the other one holding them up.

"Ah, sorry!"

"Pardon me, Kirito."

Asuna and Alice grabbed me by the back of the collar and

hauled me out of the way. If it had happened a second later, the logs would've flattened me.

So I nearly died, but Asuna had discovered a simple method to remove the obstacles blocking our way—I considered it a wash. The three of us tapped logs and absorbed them into our inventories, and in a matter of seconds, the wall was gone, but our carrying weight was over 90 percent full. We'd have to use good old-fashioned athletic maneuvering from this point on.

Fortunately, there were no more walls tall enough to need climbing over, so a sequence of hopping and ducking was enough. A few minutes later, the space ahead of us opened up much wider.

"Ah...," Asuna gasped. I couldn't tell at first if it was out of relief or shock.

The log cabin that held so many of our memories was resting in the middle of a little clearing in the forest, badly damaged.

It had escaped total destruction, but it was far from unharmed. The left wall had absorbed continual shock damage from the fall until it was utterly busted, and the roof and center of the cabin were heavily dented. Every last glass window had shattered, and the porch and front steps looked like they'd been trampled and squashed by the Deviant Gods of Jotunheim.

But considering the cabin fell from a height of thousands and thousands of feet, it was practically a miracle that it still resembled a house at all. That was probably thanks to the initial impact being absorbed by the river—and the many trees that were sacrificed to slow it down once it had skipped.

Asuna started running toward it. Alice and I followed her.

She stopped at the collapsed porch and looked up at the cabin in silence. Alice was going to say something to comfort her, then decided better of that and looked to me instead.

"Kirito...is there any way we can repair this house?"

"Repair...? The thing is, player homes are supposed to be indestructible objects...They don't have a durability rating in the first place," I said, walking over to Asuna. I tapped the railing of the porch, which was twisted diagonally. When I examined the window that popped up, I exclaimed in surprise.

In *ALO*, when you looked at the properties of a player-owned home, all it displayed was the fact that it *was* owned by a player. But this large window said *Cypress Log Cabin* at the top, followed by the owners—Asuna and me—on the next line, then a colored bar that seemed to represent a durability level. The numbers on the bar's overlay said *4,713/12,500*. That had to be the log cabin's HP.

Compared to my own HP, which was under a hundred, a total near five thousand was vast, but it was nearly at a third of its maximum value. And even as I was watching, the number ticked down to *4,712*. It seemed that damage to the very structure of the cabin caused a slow continual decrease. It was going at about one point every ten seconds, meaning we had 47,100 seconds until it reached zero. Divided by sixty, that made 785 minutes—or a bit over thirteen hours.

The clock readout in the lower-right corner said it was 5:32 PM on September 27th. If we did nothing at all, this log cabin would lose all of its durability by six thirty in the morning tomorrow—and vanish for good.

Asuna reached the same conclusion as she stared at the properties window. She murmured, "By tomorrow morning..."

Once again, however, Alice's calm observation helped to slow my rising panic. "Is that not a REPAIR button at the bottom of that window?"

"Ah!" I glanced down and saw a series of four buttons: INFO, TRANSACTION, REPAIR, and BREAK DOWN.

"Whew...," I murmured, feeling relief flood through me. I tapped the REPAIR button, being *very* careful to avoid touching the BREAK DOWN button next to it.

Unfortunately, the busted house did not glow with a miraculous light and refresh like new before our eyes. Instead, we were greeted with two cruel messages.

The Beginner Carpentry skill is required to repair this structure.

You are missing the requisite materials to repair this structure. To complete repair, you will need: sawed log × 162, sawed plank × 75, iron sheet × 216, iron nail × 463, linseed oil × 30, glass pane × 24.

"A hundred…and sixty-two…logs…"

"And what's the Carpentry skill…? Does that mean you can build your own house?" wondered Asuna, who was equally stunned. We shared a look, and I nodded awkwardly.

"I…suppose so. It's not rare among games where player housing is a big selling point, but *ALO* and *SAO* never had that system. Meaning…"

"We should consider this to be an entirely different game," said Alice crisply. She clapped her hands. "But it does mean we now know what to do. If we gather the materials listed there, and learn this Carpentry skill, we can bring this house back to life. I suppose there's no point in wasting time, is there?"

"Yeah…you're right," said Asuna, who was quick to transition to action, despite being more shaken than me by this experience. She stared at the window again, presumably memorizing the names and numbers of the items.

"First of all, for the hundred and sixty-two logs, I think we'll get them quickly. There are plenty just lying around here," she said speedily, pointing at the piles of toppled conifer trees, stacked up like boulders. She was probably correct that we could use them, but I suspected that a problem or two still needed to be dealt with first.

But we could worry about that later. I said to Asuna, "Then we should hurry up with gathering. I can't imagine those logs will stay in acceptable condition for hours and hours without degrading."

"Good point," she said.

Before she could run off, I grabbed her wrist and advised, "First, let's dump out the logs we just picked up, so we're carrying less weight to begin with."

Without a word, Asuna promptly opened her window and got

to work. Three large wooden logs settled with a thump onto the front-yard portion of the cabin, which had once been carefully manicured grass but was now covered in bushes and weeds. The jagged breaks and extra branches were cleaned up, as opposed to before we acquired them, but the bark of the tree was still rough.

Alice and I produced our logs in the same place, then brought out our weapons as well, to stand them up against the pile. I was nervous about leaving my weapon out in the open, but I couldn't imagine any players were around to steal it.

Once my inventory was empty, I sprinted back to where the trees were felled. I tapped them one after the other, selecting the option to take them into my storage. It took just five or six trees to hit my carrying capacity. At that point, I had to rush back to the cabin and take them back out.

After I'd repeated this trip five times, the space in front of the cabin was completely packed with logs. Since we were here, I went ahead and cleared some of the other felled trees around the building to free up more space. This process would be impossible in the real world without some special heavy machinery, but the exercise didn't tire out my virtual avatar. The three of us worked in silence until, twenty minutes later, all the felled trees were arranged into massive piles of neat, orderly logs.

Asuna caught her breath and pointed a finger to count them. "Let's see; one pile is fifteen logs, and there are ten piles, making a hundred and fifty...really? This much, and we're still short?!"

"By twelve," murmured Alice, shrugging. She looked around at the forest. "But there are plenty of trees all around. We can make up the difference in no time by cutting some down."

But even that's not going to be easy, I thought. Then I had a new concern.

"Before that...Asuna, what's the item name for those logs?"

"Huh...?" She tapped a nearby log skeptically. When the properties window appeared, she read aloud, "It says *aged spiral pine sawlog*. So I guess these trees are called spiral pines..."

"Do those exist in the real world?"

"No!" she said immediately, as though annoyed I would even think that. She brushed the rough bark with her palm. "But I think it's rather fine wood. I bet it would make for good lumber once it's processed."

"Ahhh…there were similar trees in the forest around Rulid," said Alice. The familiar name brought a pang of nostalgia to my throat, but I swallowed it down so I could explain my worry.

"Well, you know how it says sawlog in the name? I don't think this qualifies as the necessary type of wood to fix the cabin yet. We're going to need to process these logs into proper lumber."

"P-process…? But there are no chain saws or lumber mills in this world."

I'd never heard of a lumber mill before. In fact, I had to wonder how deep Asuna's love of wood furniture went that she knew what it was. But that was beside the point.

"No," I said, "I don't think those larger machines exist at all in this world. We should be able to turn the sawlogs into sawed logs with the right tools. And I bet the process is the same as blacksmithing and woodworking in *SAO*."

"Ohhh," Asuna exclaimed, understanding. She glanced at the mountain of logs. "As in, you just rub the proper tool against the logs a few times? So that means the question is what kind of tool is it, and how do we get it…"

"Yeah…Ahhh, if only Yui were here!"

I tried not to take advantage of the privilege of her navigation abilities on a daily basis, but I wasn't going to be shy in an emergency like this. Asuna grimaced briefly, then looked worried.

"You still can't contact her?" she asked.

"Yeah…I think the navigation pixie system from *ALO* has been entirely removed. But I couldn't guess if Yui's still the way she is with Liz's group or if she's been cut off from the server…"

I could see Asuna's expression growing gloomier as I went on, so I hastily added, "Oh, but Yui's physical hardware is in my PC at home, so there's no chance anything's *really* happened to her. If you're worried, we can log out to check on her…"

"…No, I'm fine. If she's with Liz and Silica, I'd want her to help them," Asuna said bracingly, then slapped the log next to her. "We should do what we can on our own."

"There's the Asuna I know," said Alice with a smile. She brushed the bumpy surface of the spiral pine with her gauntleted hand. "I do not know very much about the carpentry business, but when I fled Central Cathedral to the forest around Rulid, I got help from Old Man Garitta in building my own shack. I cut down pine trees like these, if not quite as large, cleared the branches, and peeled the bark to turn them into logs. But I do recall that to remove the bark, I had to use a tool like a thin, flat blade with handles on either end."

The sight of Alice moving her hands to indicate the shape of the tool made me feel self-conscious.

I'd heard what happened in the time between the battle with Administrator and the eventual Otherworld War. For about half a year, Alice took care of me in a shack she'd built in the woods outside Rulid, because my fluctlight was damaged, leaving me unconscious. Trying to imagine what state I was in, and what she had to do to take care of me, filled me with a feeling that was difficult to describe. I had to push that carefully aside for now to focus on the topic at hand.

While I couldn't envision the tool Alice was describing, Asuna knew what it was right away.

"Ah, that's a drawknife. They use them to shave off tree bark overseas. In Japan, they usually use a shaver with a long handle that looks like a farming tool."

"Hmm. Then we shall need to build or purchase this drawknife tool. But to create one would require other tools and materials, I am sure…and I did not see any towns or villages around where we fell." The cat-eared knight scowled, scratching at the stubbled bark of the spiral pine with her fingernails. "Argh! Forget the drawknife; even a regular knife would be enough for me to scrape loose this infernal bark."

I had to smile at the boldness of her claim. Asuna herself gasped, as though she just remembered something.

"H-hang on a moment!" she cried, rushing into the half-destroyed house. But she emerged in less than ten seconds, shaking her head with disappointment.

"If our home item storage was fine, I could have come out with a knife...but it's empty, just like ours. All the furniture and cutlery we had sitting in the open is gone, too."

"Okay..."

The furnishings and decorations we had in the log cabin were an elite selection that Asuna had bought from shops across Alfheim. The shock of all that effort gone in an instant had to be worse than I could imagine. I started toward Asuna, intent on comforting her, when another thought occurred to me.

"...No, wait...If a knife will work, then..."

I spun around to look at the side of a pile of logs, where four swords, a staff, and a shield were resting. I raced over and grabbed the hilt of the Blárkveld.

"...I should be able to shave down the bark on these logs."

"That might be true, Kirito, but have you forgotten the sorry mess you made of yourself earlier?" Alice wondered in exasperation.

I threw her a wicked smirk. "Of course I haven't forgotten. But I went over the weight limit because I had everything on. If I take off all my other gear..."

As I spoke, I spun my hand to bring up the ring menu, then rotated it to the equipment menu. The mannequin there, at least, was the same as since the *SAO* days—I slapped the REMOVE ALL EQUIPMENT button to the left of it. A number of circles of light surrounded my body, causing my coat, shirt, pants, and boots to instantly vanish. The only thing left was a pair of black boxers.

Instantly, the girls were shrieking.

"Wh-what do you think you're doing?!"

"Don't just strip naked out here!"

But I didn't want to waste time apologizing. "Just watch!"

I clapped my hands now that they were ungloved and grabbed Blárkveld's hilt. I dropped my center of weight and moved to pull it out in one smooth motion…

Instead, my knees hit the ground. The sword was simply resting against the logs, but it felt as heavy as if it were welded to the ground. In the real world, I could have easily thrown out my back attempting this.

"Huh…?! But why…?"

The armor I'd stripped off was basically only leather and cloth, but it was all high-level gear, so it had to be heavy. It was impossible for the combined weight of those clothes to be less than one sword.

Baffled, I stared at the sword from my knees. Then an idea struck my brain.

"Oh…d-do you think maybe it was a temporary assistance measure…?"

"What do you mean?" asked Asuna, confused.

I looked up at her and explained my conjecture. "Well…I don't know when the exact moment was, but we all got turned back to level-1 characters with our stats reset, right? I thought the reason I didn't instantly go over our weight limit from the armor was because I've been wearing leather and cloth…but Alice's armor has plenty of metal, and everyone who plays a tank would be decked out in full plate armor. It would be totally unfair if everyone like that was immediately immobilized by the weight limit after the reset."

"Well…I suppose you're right…"

"So I think there must have been some kind of assistance measure that went into effect, such that the gear you had equipped during the reset has a lowered encumbrance, meaning you can still keep it equipped without being weighed down. But we had our weapons put away in our item storage, so…"

"The weapons didn't get the effect applied to them…and that's why we can't equip them now?" said Asuna, catching on quickly. She frowned. "But wait. If that's correct…and you just unequipped all of your armor…"

"Yes," I said heavily, opening my equipment window again. In the list of items on the right side of the window, I dragged the Cloak of Harald—my main armor—onto the torso slot. The rings of light appeared, and my dark-gray coat materialized.

"Hrrg!"

I'd been preparing myself, but I still wasn't able to withstand the weight all over my body. I had to place my hands on the ground; if I kept sinking downward, it would look like I was begging Asuna in apology. With great effort, I lifted my right hand. A pop-up appeared reading *Physique skill proficiency has risen to 2*, to which I thought *Oh, shut up!* and then pushed the REMOVE ALL EQUIPMENT button again. The torturous weight vanished, and I exhaled again.

"…And there you have it," I said, lifting my face and grinning.

There was a thunderclap behind me. "Are you an absolute fool?!"

Alice lined up next to Asuna, her golden armor clattering, and jabbed an accusing finger at me where I knelt, dressed in nothing but my boxers.

"Why did you not realize this before you removed all your clothing?! Now you will be forced to walk about in this pathetic state for the time being!" she hissed.

"Well, um, yeah," I admitted, grimacing. I hoisted myself up to my feet. "But at least I'm the only victim. It would be a disaster if you two had stripped down, too."

"If that happened, I would not log in again until you had prepared new clothes for us," Alice said bluntly, causing Asuna to suddenly burst into laughter.

"You two always act this way," she said, giggling and shaking her head. That was enough to disengage Alice from her scolding mode, but it didn't solve our problem.

"So the swords won't help us…which leaves…"

I folded my arms and thought it over.

We were level-1 again, with all of our stats reset, almost all of our items lost, and even a UI change, but at the very least, we were still in a VRMMO. That part was beyond all doubt. But it was seeming to me like the abbreviation at the end of that term should be different now. We had gone from a VRMMORPG to a different genre.

"*Survival…*," I muttered. The two girls looked at me with suspicion.

"What did you say?"

"I think this might be a survival game…"

"…*Survival*? What do you mean?" asked Alice. The word I spoke was English, which she understood as the sacred tongue in the Underworld. Her recent experiences had given her plenty of practice with English, but this reference was lost on her.

"It's a genre of games. Originally, survival games were something you did in the real world with air guns—weapons for fun—but lately there's been a growing genre of computer games by the same name. Some people call them open-world survival games. They're more difficult to play than ordinary RPGs—the conditions of survival are harsher, and the penalty is worse."

"What do you mean by conditions of survival?"

"For example, you don't die in *ALO* even if you never eat or drink anything, remember? But survival games have hunger and thirst meters, so your HP goes down if you don't drink water or eat food. Oh! That's why…"

At last, I recognized the purpose of the two extra bars below HP and MP.

"Between the blue TP bar and yellow SP bar, one of them must be hunger, and the other one must be thirst."

Asuna immediately said, "In that case, TP must stand for thirst points and SP for stamina points."

"Ah. G-got it."

"Hmm," Alice murmured, putting a slender hand to her throat. "But despite running back and forth with those logs, I haven't felt the tiniest bit hungry or thirsty, and the two bars haven't dipped at all."

"I think there's a grace period with that, just like with the equipment weight."

"Oh?"

"The basic structure of survival games is that, when you die, you drop all your items and have to go back to retrieve them after you revive. It wouldn't exactly be fair to put players in this unfamiliar world without a manual—and have them immediately starve to death and lose their gear...I'm betting the TP bar will start to dip first. Though I don't know if there will be any actual sensation of thirst to go with it."

As I explained, I could feel myself sinking into a deeper, heavier feeling. I put my hands on my hips and exhaled slowly. At the moment, I was dressed in nothing but my underwear, unable to use my sword and armor. It didn't feel like I was going to be surviving long.

But I told myself, "That doesn't mean I can just sit here feeling sorry for myself...I can't just go off dying without finding out who completely overwrote this world and why. Plus, I want to restore our home to its proper state."

"That's the spirit, Kirito," said Alice with a fierce grin. She reached out and slapped me on the bare back.

It didn't hurt, but out of pure instinct, I yelped, "Ouch!"

"I don't know much about this survival genre, but of course I felt hunger and thirst within the Underworld. Just look around us...there's a river right over there—and fruit and beasts in the forest. If you starve among bounty like this, the goblins in the Dark Territory would laugh at you."

"......W-well, I guess you're right..."

I wasn't sure if they should be compared directly, but it was true that this forest seemed unimaginably lush in comparison to the misery of the Dark Territory in the Underworld. Our log cabin could have gotten tossed into the barren deserts of the salamander territory of Alfheim, so this had to be a pretty cushy starting location for a survival game.

I stretched up tall and gazed at the sky, which was growing golden. After a moment, I sucked in a deep breath and announced, "All right...I don't know what this game is called, but I can tell it's not a VRMMORPG anymore, but a VRMMO survival game. I'll eat rocks if that's what it takes to survive, until I've built the Kirito Empire upon this soil!"

Ooh! the girls exclaimed—but only in my dreams.

In reality, Asuna merely gave me an awkward look and said, "Well, um, I'll just be happy with protecting our home."

Alice looked as annoyed as she could possibly be and added, "Nothing you say can possibly sound as bold and inspiring as you hope when you're dressed like that."

3

And so it was that my survival declaration did not come off as impressively as I had intended. Regardless, I still managed to gaze around the clearing with a renewed sense of spirit.

The grassy area the half-busted log cabin fit neatly into was a circle about fifty feet across. It was originally surrounding a mega-sized spiral pine, I decided, but now sported a fresh footpath to the southwest that ended at the river. The empty space of the clearing was stuffed full of 150 logs, and our first task was to do something about it.

My only experience with survival-type RPGs was on my old PC years ago, so I had no experience with them in a full-dive setting; but the general strategy should still be the same. First you acquired water and food, then found tools and materials, so you could create garments, shelter, and weapons.

But in this initial grace period, we wouldn't get hungry or thirsty, plus there was a river nearby, so we could worry about that part later. The first task for us was gaining the most primitive of tools: a knife.

"Let's go back to the river."

"Why? To catch fish?" Asuna wondered, wide-eyed.

I gave her a toothy grin. "Eventually. But there's something else to do first."

We trotted down the path freshly cleared of felled trees toward the river. The bank, which was littered with stones of many colors, seemed difficult to walk on before, but now that I was looking at it through the lens of a survival game, I realized it was a mountain of treasure. I stopped and told the girls, "Look for as heavy and hard of a rock as you can. Preferably long and narrow, about twelve inches."

"…Got it." Alice and Asuna walked away, looking down at their feet, while I turned my back to search for something else. I wanted a large rock with a flat, stable top—a workstation. I found a good one right away, so I picked up a random round stone off the ground and smashed it against the rock surface. It split into two pieces on the first hit. If this were an ordinary VRM-MORPG, the shattered rock would spray off light particles and vanish, but the two pieces resting on top of the work surface were not going away. I tapped them to check the properties. It said: *Cracked Favillite, Weapon/Material, Attack Power: 2.18 striking, Durability: 5.44, Weight: 3.71.*

"Ugh…It even goes down to decimal points," I groaned, just in time to hear footsteps and voices behind me.

"How about this one?" "Will this work?"

Asuna placed a rough, gray-green rock on my workstation. Alice rolled a smooth, blackish-brown stone next to it. Both were the size and shape I'd asked for.

"Let's see…"

I picked them up, one in each hand, and gauged their weight. Both felt very solid and heavy, but the green one was just a tad more so. On the other hand, I felt like the black one was harder.

For now, I decided on using the green one as material, placing it in the middle of the slab and holding it there with my left hand. I lifted the black stone in my right and took careful aim. Whether in the real or virtual world, losing your concentration during tasks like this was cause for error. I shouted "Three, two, one!" and swung it down with all my strength.

Clang! Orange sparks shot outward from the collision. Carefully, I let go with my left hand—the green stone sat there briefly, then split down the middle. There was a dull shine to the split face, and the edge was as sharp as a shard of glass.

"That's pretty good," I murmured to myself, holding one of the halves and raising the black stone again. I focused on a spot next to the split edge and swung again. But this time I didn't get enough on it. There were only a few sparks, and nothing happened.

"Um, Kirito?" asked Asuna at my right while I was aiming for my third strike. "I get what you're trying to do…but when you're banging rocks together while dressed like that…Well…"

She had her hands pressed to her mouth for some reason. Then Alice pointed out, "You look like the Neanderthals on the TV show I saw the other day. What if you wear a pelt instead of your underwear?"

Asuna lost control and started giggling, and Alice followed her lead. And here I was in my underwear, doing my best to help them survive.

"Hohhh! Hoh-hoh-hoh! Hoh-hoh-hoh-hohhh!" I grunted, pretending. Instantly, the floodgates burst open, and the girls grabbed their sides and howled with laughter. While they shrieked, I lifted up my striking stone again.

"Hohhh!!" I bellowed, smashing the green rock, right next to the previous split, and creating another fine vertical crack. A thin layer of stone broke free and landed on the stone slab. It was about a foot long, two inches wide, and less than half an inch thick…exactly the shape I was looking for.

I brushed the other pieces off to the side and laid the shard flat on the work surface. One end was thinner than the other, so I decided that would be the tip, and the thicker side would be the handle. Very carefully, I struck it with the black stone.

This was a virtual world, so I had faith that the system would understand my intention and fashion the stone into the shape I was envisioning. Even still, I was very cautious about how I struck it. Eventually, just for an instant, the stone shard shone.

A system window popped up before my eyes.

Stoneworking skill gained. Proficiency has risen to 1.

Earning a new skill was always cause for celebration, but I was more curious about the quality of my finished product. I tapped the stone shard, which was now in roughly the right shape, calling up its window.

Crude Viridacutite Knife, Weapon/Tool, Attack Power: 7.82 slashing, 5.33 piercing, Durability: 10.05, Weight: 3.53.

"Yesss!" I shouted, striking a pose. I'd forgotten about the Neanderthal act. It said *crude*, but the attack power and durability were significantly higher than the cracked favillite I'd made earlier. This would make the job much easier.

I placed the knife at the edge of the workspace, then gathered the pieces of the rock that was apparently called viridacutite. Once again, I struck it with the black rock. The piece that chipped off was too small, so I tried again. After a couple of attempts, I got a good-sized slice, so I chipped down the right details and produced a second knife.

Either because my Stoneworking skill was already at 3 thanks to the extra practice or because my own ability as a player was getting better, the third one was done very quickly. The remaining piece of viridacutite, apparently under the size necessary for a modified item to exist, vanished into little dots of light.

I laid out the three knives on the stone work surface.

Whether VR or traditional, games treated weapons and tools with a simple general rule: If it has the same name, it has the same shape. It made sense, given that you're creating multiple copies of the same in-game object, but because the chips and dents are also matching, it made for an odd visual effect when the identical pieces were laid side by side.

These three knives, however, while essentially the same size and shape, were all different in the fine way they had broken off, the contours of the edges, and the coloring. I checked their windows—they were all considered viridacutite knives, but the attack and durability ratings also had different decimal values.

"Hmm…"

I looked down at the countless rocks beneath my feet, then at the afternoon sky overhead.

A server having a number of unique rare weapons was one thing, but if they had more than three sets of visual data for the lowliest stone knife, that was a very thorough level of in-game assets—and it only made the situation eerier. No matter how excellent The Seed Package might be for VR game development, the costs of producing this level of detail had no upper limit. At the very least, whoever had sucked the *ALO* players into this survival game was clearly not very interested in the cost efficiency of this game as a product.

A creator like Seijirou Kikuoka, who had built the Underworld, or Akihiko Kayaba, who had built Aincrad.

"Do you not like how they look, Kirito?"

Asuna was leaning over to question me, and I raised my head with a start. I pushed that disquieting thought away and shook my head. "N-no, it's not that. Um, I was just wondering if, uh, there's a way to upgrade these further…"

It was a spontaneous excuse to hide my real thoughts, but once I said it, I realized it was worth trying out. Processing and customizing items was a major facet of survival games. I looked around the area for a bundle of weeds sticking out of some rocks and used one of the new stone knives to cut the bundle loose. I gave one end of the bundle to Asuna to hold, then twisted it. Once the twists reached from end to end, the weeds shone like the knife did, and another new message appeared.

Weaving skill gained. Proficiency has risen to 1.

Yeah, yeah, I'll take a look later, I thought, closing the window so I could tap the freshly woven grass rope.

Crude Ubiquigrass Rope, Tool/Material, Durability: 4.10, Weight: 0.65.

Once again, it was crude, but I just needed it to be usable. I picked up a knife from the workspace and wrapped the grass rope tightly around the handle end. As I hoped, the item flashed again when I was done wrapping, and the rope fused to the knife, despite the fact that I didn't tie a knot at the end.

Crude Rope-Wrapped Viridacutite Knife, Weapon/Tool, Attack Power: 7.82 slashing, 5.33 piercing, Durability: 15.82, Weight: 4.18.

"And that's how it works," I said, showing them the properties window. They nodded, half impressed by my handiwork.

"I see. So the upgrade increased the durability…"

"With a bit of a bump in weight, however."

I was hoping for at least a polite round of applause, but I was disappointed. Asuna and Alice looked at each other and offered their thoughts simultaneously.

"How annoying!"

"It seems like a very tiresome process."

I made the two annoyed girls create their own grass ropes so that they learned the Weaving skill, and we returned to the log cabin carrying our new stone knives.

At this point, the crimson of the sunset sky was directly overhead. It would be dark within an hour. It seemed impossible for us to gather all the necessary supplies for repair by then, but I at least wanted to get the logs done.

This will work, I told myself, placing my other hand on a nearby log and sinking the edge of the knife into the rough bark. By rubbing it back and forth vigorously, I created a pleasant ripping sound, tearing the bark loose to fall to the ground, where it…did *not* disappear. Once again, there was a window right in front of my face.

Woodworking skill gained. Proficiency has risen to 1.

I was expecting that to happen, so I erased it at once and ignored the bark on the ground for now, focusing on moving the knife. If you tried to shave a tree trunk this size with a knife barely better than a Stone Age tool, it would take you more than an entire day, but in the virtual world, as long as the *way* you did it was right, the rest of the process was simplified—in most cases. The thick bark fell away with enjoyable regularity, and in just a minute, the blackened spiral pine sawlog flashed and turned into a rounded ivory-white bare log.

Shallow grooves ran all over the shining inner wood in spirals and swirls, which I guessed was the root of its name. I tapped the surface, and the window that appeared revealed the new item as *Sawed Aged Spiral Pine Log*. The repair window for the cabin didn't specify a tree species, so that should meet the requirements.

"Do you get how this works?" I asked the other two.

Asuna and Alice nodded.

"Then help me strip the bark off all these logs."

We got right to it. With the three of us working together, the 150 logs represented about fifty minutes of work.

But that wasn't all of it. Aside from the sawed logs, we needed seventy-five sawed planks, two hundred iron sheets, a bunch of iron nails, oil, and glass…It was obviously impossible for us to gather all these things before nightfall. The planks were one thing, but creating the iron sheets and nails from scratch would require a variety of raw materials and quality tools and fixtures, plus the skill proficiency to use them.

I really need a wiki! I thought desperately as my hands busied themselves hacking off tree bark. Under normal circumstances, running around to gather information on my own and brainstorming with friends to complete a goal was the entire point of an RPG—but with our log cabin scheduled to fall apart in half a day, I was desperate for any help I could get. If I had access to a wiki right now, that would be the cat's meow. Actually, one of us *was* technically a cat. Would that be the "cait sith's meow," then? They'd probably been telling that joke since *ALO* launched, so I decided it was best not to try that one out on my captive audience.

Such wandering thoughts filled my mind while my hands were busy. The work itself was moving smoothly, but I was worried about the durability of the stone knife I was abusing. It was a crude knife, after all, so I wouldn't be surprised if that durability rating of 15 went down to zero at any moment. If I stopped and checked its properties, I'd know the number right away, but it wasn't like I had any way to make it last longer, so I chose to focus on the task at hand instead, praying it would hold out. Every now and then, a window appeared to let me know that my Wood-working proficiency had risen, which was the encouragement I needed to keep going.

I had estimated fifty minutes, but by getting accustomed to the action over time, we reached the final log at just forty-two. Asuna and Alice finished skinning their fiftieth logs a bit before me, which didn't feel fair, but at least I could thank my knife for holding up throughout the task.

The tree trunk flashed and turned into a sawed log, and I gave my stone knife a tap. The window said that its remaining durability rating was only 0.46.

"Ooh, yours just barely made it," said Alice. She checked her own knife. It said 0.13.

"Wrapping the rope around it was the right call," said Asuna with a grin that faded quickly. She'd probably remembered that we had only finished acquiring one of the six different materials needed for the task. And the trees we'd used to get them weren't even ones we'd cut down ourselves—they had been knocked flat by the falling island. We'd need at least an ax to cut down more trees for the remaining twelve logs and all the planks.

"…Another twelve hours…," she murmured worriedly.

I had to add another cruel fact to the picture. "And…tomorrow's Monday…"

"Ah!"

Asuna's eyes bulged; she'd forgotten that part. If we were heading into Saturday or Sunday, we could have attempted to pull an all-nighter collecting materials, but staying in a dive right up until leaving for school was too much to ask. I might be able to do something like that, but a good daughter from a rich family wouldn't get away with such behavior. She'd just made up with her strict mother; she didn't need to get in trouble for playing games all night.

I placed a hand on her shoulder and willed as much reassurance as I could into my voice. "It'll be all right. If my parents find out, I can get down on my hands and knees to beg their forgiveness—I'll find a way to gather all the materials tonight and save our cabin. Trust in me; I'll get it done."

"And I will help, of course. I have nothing on my schedule until tomorrow evening," added Alice with a smile, but it did not cheer Asuna up.

"...But...it won't be easy to make iron and glass, will it? If the three of us work together to the last moment and it doesn't work out, I can probably accept that defeat...but I can't log out early and leave you two to do the hardest parts on your own..."

"..."

I was going to reassure her again but thought better of it. In the reverse situation, I would probably log out and then be up all night, unable to sleep. As a matter of fact, our probability of getting all the materials in twelve hours was very low. In that situation, I would rather have her stay than drive her out. But...

"Hmm..."

I could practically feel the smoke gushing from my ears, I was thinking so hard. Almost without realizing I was doing it, I asked, "Your mom...How is Kyouko keeping track of your diving?"

"Well, she has an admin screen for our home server. She's not totally monitoring me like before, but she does stay up late working...so if she happens to glance at the screen, she'll know right away."

"Hmm, I see...All right, I'll do something about that."

"Wh-what?! How?!" Asuna asked, shocked.

I grinned. "I'll let that be a surprise for later...In any case, you'll need to log off for dinner, right?"

"Yeah...from around seven to seven thirty."

"Okay, I'll log off at the same time. I'll send you a message after."

"All right…," Asuna said, but there was still apprehension in her eyes as she looked to the log cabin and went silent.

The left wall was completely collapsed, the ceiling was heavily dented, and the framework was bent. It hurt just to look at it like this. Every second that passed, our home's durability ticked away.

I was going to tell her once again that it was all going to be okay, but first, Alice held her stomach and complained, "If only my machine body were able to eat food already."

Asuna and I were taken by surprise. "Um…you mean, like, normal bread and rice and meat and stuff…?" I asked.

The cat-eared knight nodded matter-of-factly. "Yes, of course. According to Dr. Koujiro and Higa, development is proceeding. Apparently, fine-tuning the taste sensors and such will take more time."

"Ooh!" Asuna exclaimed, smiling at last. She reached out to grab Alice's hand and shouted, "Then when you're able to eat food in the real world, we'll have to throw you a welcoming party at Dicey Café! I'll make lots of delicious food for the occasion!"

"That is a very enticing offer. I will have to rush Higa."

The two women were so excited about this that all I could think at the moment was *Good luck, Higa.*

The sky was turning deep purple at this point, with stars peeking through. It was 6:50 PM, about time for us to log out of this mystery world—but there was something I wanted to try first.

Asuna, Alice, and I split up the ten piles of sawed aged spiral pine logs between our three personal inventories. Once we were full, we rushed into the log cabin and moved them to the home storage, a large decorative box attached to the wall of the living room. While the life span of the building itself might have been dropping, it still functioned as a home, so even on the off chance that some other players happened across our cabin while we were offline, they wouldn't be able to get inside, much less steal our precious logs.

When the 150 logs were stored inside the cabin, we picked up all the loose bark that was still lying around, and despite not knowing what it might be used for, we stored that, too. Lastly, we packed away the weapons that were unusable for the moment and headed for the living room. It was 6:55 PM now.

The next time I log in, I need some new armor...or at least clothes, I thought, looking down at my nearly naked avatar.

Then I glanced at Asuna and Alice. "See you in thirty minutes."

"...Yeah."

I hadn't explained the nature of my secret plan to Asuna, but the fencer responded bravely anyway. Alice nodded without a word, and the three of us called up the ring menu together. The SYSTEM icon was in the upper left, and from the submenu that followed, we pressed the LOG OUT button with a door icon on it.

A confirmation window appeared with a little jingle. It warned that if you didn't log out in a safe location, you could possibly die while in the middle of the process, but there was no safer place to be than inside a player-owned home.

I hit the check-mark-shaped button at the bottom of the window, and the text at the top of the confirmation window changed.

Disconnecting from Unital Ring.

"*Unital...Ring?*" I repeated. That was the very first time I'd heard the name of this world.

So we weren't in Alfheim anymore. It was an unfamiliar place ruled by a completely new game system.

A rainbow ring rose up from my feet, surrounding my avatar and covering the evening scene with a deluge of color. I was lifted by a sense of weightlessness, the direction of gravity shifting...

When I regained the sensation of my physical body, I couldn't yet open my eyes.

The pressure of the mattress against my back, the softness of the pillow supporting my head, and the rougher fiber of the mattress-pad texture against my hands were all the familiar sensations of my own bed. The LOG OUT button was functioning properly.

Relieved, I was about to open my eyes when I noticed something.

There was a considerable weight against my stomach. In fact, I felt the sides of my body being compressed, too.

Am I tied down?! I thought in a panic, tearing the AmuSphere off my head and opening my eyes.

"Ah, you're awake!" said a voice.

I wasn't being restrained. Someone was straddling my stomach. The room was somewhat dark, so I couldn't see a face, but there was only one person in the entire world whom I knew would do something like this.

"...Um...Suguha?" I said to my sister. "What are you doing there?"

"You shouldn't have to ask. It's almost dinnertime, so I came to wake you up!" Suguha pouted, puffing her cheeks. She reached out with an arm encased in a track jacket sleeve and tugged on my bangs. "I shook you and shook you, but you wouldn't wake up, so I was almost about to rip your AmuSphere off. Even in combat, you should have noticed!"

"No, I wasn't in combat...Hmm, that's weird. I didn't feel any shaking at all. Anyway, you don't have to be physical about it; you could have just sent me a message."

ALO allowed for communication with outside networks, which meant you could browse the Net while in-game, trade e-mails, and send short messages. But Suguha pouted even more and protested, "I did! Twice! But minutes went by without any contact, so I had to resort to more direct measures!"

"Wait, really? I didn't get anything."

"You were probably so wrapped up in your questing that you didn't even notice. Ugh, if I'd gotten back an hour earlier, I could have joined everyone. Liz was supposed to show me a great new spot for raising skill levels that she was telling me about..."

"They invited me, too, but I definitely got Liz's message. Must have been some system error or disconnection…," I started to say, before I thought better of it.

It wasn't an error that Suguha's messages didn't reach me. By that point, the game system had already transitioned over—from the familiar style of *ALfheim Online* to this mysterious new survival RPG, *Unital Ring*. Apparently, *UR*—if that was how they officially abbreviated it—was not nearly as welcoming of outside connections as *ALO*.

"…I think you made the right decision not diving in, Sugu," I muttered.

My sister blinked. "What do you mean by that?"

"Um…it's hard to explain briefly, but something bad is happening inside…"

"Bad? Like a salamander attack?"

"No, not that sort of thing. I'm still not quite sure *what's* hap—"

I cut myself off there. Asuna and Alice should have logged out safely by now, like me. But what about Liz, Silica, and Yui, who were on the forty-fifth floor of New Aincrad when the anomaly happened?

I did a sit-up to get off my back, and it caused Suguha to topple off her mounted position and onto her back.

"Aaagh!" she shrieked, flopping her legs in the air, but I ignored my sister and grabbed the Augma off the desk and put it on. As soon as it was active, I shouted, "Yui, are you there?!"

But there was no response. She was probably still in *ALO*…er, in *Unital Ring*. If I wanted, I could use the PC where Yui's core program was stored to shut off her connection to the game, but I didn't want to force her to do anything unless it was absolutely necessary.

"But what does it mean…?" I muttered to myself.

Then something clicked in my mind.

The fact that I could log out meant that *Unital Ring* wasn't shut off from the rest of the world like the old *SAO*. The abnormal event happened around five o'clock in the afternoon, and it was almost seven now. Over the past two hours, many of those *ALO* players must have logged out and talked to the publisher or traded information elsewhere online.

Using the virtual desktop my Augma displayed, I tried to access the biggest online game info site in the country, MMO Today. But just then, Suguha stood furiously at my side, having rolled backward off the bed to escape, and yanked on my shirt.

"I told you, it's dinnertime! Mom made your favorite tonight!"

Well, now I couldn't tell her I'd eat later. Reluctantly, I got to my feet, still wearing the Augma.

As I walked down the hall, I opened a browser. First, I checked for messages from Ymir, the company that ran *ALO*, but there was nothing. Then I went to MMO Today, and when I glanced at the familiar top page, I squawked, "Nwuh…?!"

Suguha, who was leading the way, turned back in confusion. "What's wrong?"

But I couldn't open my mouth to speak—or even look at my sister. My body was frozen like stone, staring at the headline at the top of the web page.

Massive Abnormalities Unfolding in Over One Hundred VRMMO Worlds!

It wasn't just *ALO*.

The anomaly was happening across the entire Seed Nexus.

4

Something's wrong with you, Keiko.

That was what a friend from elementary school had said when the two of them had run into each other at random at a train station the previous week. They'd agreed to go for tea and caught up with each other, and that was when the topic of *ALO* had arisen.

Her friend's expression had been serious. She wasn't teasing, and she wasn't disillusioned; she was sincerely worried.

But even then, all that Keiko Ayano, aka Silica, could do was smile awkwardly. She knew from experience with her parents and counselors that the more she tried to explain how she felt, the bigger the gap between them would become.

You were stuck in bed for two whole years because of that whole crazy thing, and now you're back to playing VR games again. Something's wrong with you.

In an objective sense, her friend was probably right. Many people believed that every last *SAO* Survivor should despise the full-dive interface that locked them in that VRMMO and never approach such a thing again. She wasn't going to complain about that viewpoint. In fact, there were plenty of students at the special school for *SAO* Survivors who had sworn off VR games for good.

But Keiko didn't want to do that.

That was all it came down to, so why wouldn't people leave her alone about it?

Despite all that's happened, I still like playing full-dive games, she mumbled, but her friend had persisted, asking her to explain it. The school counselor had said the same thing, and so did her parents.

She couldn't explain it. Even Keiko didn't know where this feeling was coming from, shining with light from deep in her chest, igniting longing and anxiousness. She felt bad that she kept worrying her parents, and she was deeply grateful to them for not trying to force her away from VR games, but that was why she didn't want to answer the question with clichés.

There was something there.

If you boiled it down to the deepest point, that was probably it.

Full-dive VR worlds had *something* in them that drew Keiko to them. She wanted to know what that was, but she didn't need to understand it. She just wanted to feel its existence. Now and forever. No matter what happened.

That was what she told herself, but…

"…I don't think I ever expected this to happen, Pina," Silica whispered. The little baby-blue dragon on her head chirped in response. Lisbeth was weaving dried grass a little ways away; she looked up and asked, "Did you say something?"

Silica shook her head. "No. Nothing."

"Oh…"

Normally, Lisbeth would persist until she found out what was bothering Silica, but this time she just went back to her labor. She had to be really tired by now.

The black-haired little girl working diligently next to her beamed. "We can do this, Liz! If we just make twenty-two more ropes and sixteen more dried-grass bundles, and find forty-five more sturdy branches, we're done collecting materials!"

"…Y-yeah…," mumbled Lisbeth, her expression going blank when she heard the actual numbers left.

The three of them were sitting in a circle, inside a depression at the foot of a cliff. It wasn't far enough in to be a cave, but it was about ten feet deep and six feet tall, so it made for a good temporary shelter. And there was fresh underground water dripping from a crack in the back wall, too. A little fire built of dried branches crackled in their midst.

They were surrounded by arid wasteland and hadn't found a single source of water on their trek here. The dripping of water happened about once every two seconds, but when their thirst points started dropping, they couldn't be choosy about it. They needed to build up some means of survival as soon as possible.

In keeping with this line of thought, Lisbeth slapped her cheeks with both hands and exclaimed, "Yeah, we've survived this far! Let's not get down now, Silica!"

In response, Silica raised the rope she'd just finished making. "I've been working hard this whole time! This is the fourteenth one!"

"What?! You're not gonna beat me!"

Lisbeth began working her hands with a renewed fervor, while the black-haired girl, Yui the artificial intelligence, pumped an adorable little fist toward the night sky outside the hollow and cheered, "That's the spirit, Liz and Silica!"

Three hours had already passed since the mystery incident that hit *ALO*, sending the floating castle New Aincrad crashing to earth and completely altering the game system. It was eight o'clock in the real world.

When New Aincrad stopped floating and started falling, Silica, Lisbeth, and Yui were in a canyon at the edge of the forty-fifth floor. The snail-type monsters there bearing rock shells were really hardy but had low attack power, which made them perfect for skill leveling.

They had been working on their weapon skills and getting ready to leave the canyon to take a break to wait for Kirito's group to show up when the ground began violently trembling. They'd hastily spread their wings and leaped into the air but hadn't realized the entire structure of New Aincrad was falling, and they collided with the bottom of the floor above.

By following Yui's orders, they made it to the outer aperture somehow and did their best to get away from the falling castle, but they had distanced themselves no more than a hundred yards when New Aincrad crashed into land behind them with all the force of the Tunguska event. Silica held Pina and Lisbeth held Yui as the shock wave threw them through the air to land in a barren landscape they didn't recognize.

It had taken about fifteen minutes for them to confirm they weren't in salamander or imp territory, their stats had been completely reset, their wings and all items except for main weapons and armor were gone, and that Yui had lost her navigation pixie capabilities. The three of them plus Pina wandered the wilderness in search of water and shelter, until they'd found the overhang about an hour ago.

Silica and Lisbeth had both logged out once already, gone to the bathroom and replenished their fluids, so they knew this new world wasn't some inescapable death game like *SAO*. But they also discovered new problems in doing so—like *ALO*, logging out while still in the open left your avatar in place for a certain amount of time.

In the area around the hollow prowled dangerous giant scorpions and sand-colored wolves that were much too tough to be starter-zone monsters; if their empty avatars were discovered by these predators, they wouldn't last more than a few seconds. Until they knew exactly what death meant in this game—whether simply returning to a resurrection point or more severe consequences like losing experience, money, or items—they wanted to avoid losing all their HP.

So they took the pre-log-out warning seriously—*If you do not log out in a safe location, you may die while disconnecting*—and made it their first priority to acquire that safe location. Liz happened to discover the Beginner Carpentry skill and, upon activating it, saw a single name in the structures category: something called a crude hut.

"Here I was, planning to buy that same old two-story shop with a waterwheel from *SAO* when the forty-eighth floor opened up...and now I'm trying to build a crude hut," Lisbeth grumbled, looking out of their little hollow in the rock. The sun had gone down, and there was no light out in the wilderness.

"I wonder what happened to New Aincrad," murmured Silica.

Yui stopped working and looked away, her long eyelashes downcast. "At the moment New Aincrad made contact with the ground, I still had access to the map data...and everything from the first to the twenty-fifth floor was completely obliterated."

The mention of the twenty-fifth floor caused Silica to gasp. Lisbeth twitched visibly. But Yui quietly continued.

"The floors that escaped total destruction were still partially damaged in places. I also detected that about twelve hundred of the *ALO* players still inside the structure of New Aincrad died upon impact."

Silica simply stared, taking in the enormity of that statement.

A part of her had been hoping that this was all a dramatic surprise story event, but hearing that over a thousand players died eliminated that possibility for good. This was still the grace period, so she assumed the dead had been revived without a harsh penalty, but beyond that, it was too far outside the bounds of being a scripted game event.

When Yui resumed weaving her grass, Lisbeth asked hesitantly, "Um, Yui...you lost your powers around the same time that we lost our wings, right?"

"That's correct," said the girl in the little white dress. "It was at precisely 17:05 on September twenty-seventh that a number of phenomena occurred at once. The hexagonal pattern that appeared five minutes prior vanished, all the in-game UI systems changed, my system access privileges were revoked, and my avatar transformed from pixie to human. According to the game system, I am now classified as a player, like you. I have no special capabilities..."

The little girl hung her head. Silica reached out as far as she could and wrapped her hand around Yui's shoulder. "It'll be all right, Yui. I'm sure we'll find a way to get you back to normal."

"...Thank you. I'm sorry for worrying you," the AI said, bowing. To their surprise, she mumbled, "The truth is...a part of me is a little happy about this situation."

"H-happy? Why?"

"Now I can carry items and equip weapons and armor. I have an HP bar. If I lose all my HP, I'll die like you. It's not clear what will happen after that, but for the first time, I'm another VRMMO player...I'm in the same position as you and Papa and Mama. I'm scared of losing HP, but even that fear is a new and fascinating sensation for me."

It was hard for Silica to understand exactly what all these things were supposed to mean, but a part of her understood perfectly.

Yui had always been an observer of everything—from *SAO*, to *ALO*, to the Ordinal Scale incident, to even the Otherworld War in the Underworld. At last, things were different in the mysterious new world of *Unital Ring*. She had a human-sized avatar—though still smaller than even Silica's—with four new status bars. She'd lose TP when she was thirsty, SP when she was hungry, and HP when she was hurt. Yui wasn't an observer anymore. She was one of the protagonists of this world.

"...Then we'd better find you some good weapons and armor!" Lisbeth said, brandishing her newly woven rope like a sword.

She and Silica were still wearing their weapons and armor from *ALO*. It was how they were able to defeat the scorpions and camel spiders that attacked in the wilderness, but all Yui had was a thin dress, which was basically no defense at all. And if Yui's guess that they were in a temporary grace period was correct, it was quite possible that Silica and Lisbeth would be over-encumbered when it ended and no longer able to equip their gear. It was clear that they needed equipment for the three of them.

"But first, we need to get ourselves a home!" Silica insisted.

Lisbeth snorted mightily. "I just finished my twentieth one of these."

"What…? When did you get past me?"

Impressed by her friend the crafter, Silica worked feverishly on her task. When you wove the dried grass from end to end, the whole thing flashed faintly and turned into a firm rope. Yui finished her task at about the same time, which meant that of the items they needed for the hut, they'd put together the sixty crude whithergrass ropes.

If she tapped the freshly made rope, the properties window included a brief description beneath the item name and durability meter.

A crude, narrow rope woven from whithergrass, which grows in arid regions. It is tough but susceptible to dampness. The Bashin people are said to boil and eat them.

"I guess this means that if you make a rope with other kinds of grass, the properties will change," Silica murmured.

Lisbeth looked over her shoulder to read it and said, "Hmm…I suppose so. Ugh, this game is so much work…And I *really* don't want to eat these…"

"I agree with you on both points."

Yui giggled at the two of them. The mention of Bashin people in the text was curious, but she banished the thought from her mind to focus on the task at hand.

"Well, now we need sixteen bundles of dried grass…"

"And forty-five sturdy branches. We'll have to go gathering supplies again," said Lisbeth gloomily, looking out of the hollow.

Normally, if you went outdoors in the middle of the night in VRMMORPGs, it was never truly dark. There was always some level of ambient lighting in *SAO* and *ALO*, enough to see the contours of the ground at the very least. But this place was as dark as the real world was at night. If they went out without a light, they could easily tumble off a cliff without even realizing it was there.

Lisbeth raised her right hand and enunciated familiar spell words.

"Ek skapa ljós!"

That was the elementary spell for light, something most players in *ALO* had memorized. But unsurprisingly, there was no ball of light in her hand, nor even a puff of black smoke for failure. Lisbeth sighed, turned around, and shrugged.

"There's magic here, too, right?"

"There's an MP bar, so I would assume so…but I have no idea how you actually use it," said Silica, shrugging, too. Her hands fell onto her lap.

Many VRMMORPGs allowed players to use magic, but their execution fell into three broad categories. You could speak Spell-words aloud as in *ALO*, perform physical gestures with your hand or staff, or simply select them from a magical grimoire or holo-window. If it used words or gestures, they'd never guess them at random, and they had no spellbooks on hand.

"I suspect there will be an NPC who will teach the Magic skill—or something of that nature. Magic will have to wait until then," Yui said. Silica nodded in agreement.

If they couldn't use magic, it was tempting to wait until it got light out, but if this world was on *ALO*'s sixteen-hour day, they'd have to wait six hours until morning. On a twenty-four-hour day, that would be more like ten hours. It was very possible their grace period would end before then, so they needed to risk danger and leave the hollow to gather the other materials.

Silica reached out and pulled a longer branch from their little campfire. She tapped the safe end of the twig with the weak little flame at the tip.

Burning Thin Branch, Weapon/Material, Attack Power: 0.43 striking, 0.37 burning, Durability: 1.44, Weight: 0.69.

The durability number was decreasing by 0.01 about every two seconds. It would burn up in less than five minutes. It wouldn't be much good as a torch if it couldn't last at least twice that long, and the light it offered was weak, to boot.

"Um…how is a torch different from a regular branch again?" Silica wondered. Lisbeth just inclined her head in confusion. Fortunately, Yui could provide an answer.

"A torch is a stick with the end wrapped in a cloth soaked in flammable solution."

"Flammable…solution…?"

"Usually oil or sap. The Japanese word for torch is written with the kanji for *pine* and *light* because they traditionally used turpentine, which is distilled from pine trees."

Lisbeth looked at Yui with amazement. "Yui…did you just search for that information?"

"No. I cannot connect to the external Internet right now…It is information saved in my primary memory space."

"Whoa…," Lisbeth gasped. She walked over to Yui and ruffled her hair with both hands. "You really are amazing, Yui! Even without your navigation, you can help in so many ways. You should be more proud of yourself!"

"Heh…heh-heh…" Yui giggled awkwardly, unsure. "But…just knowing how torches were made doesn't help us very much in this case. We don't have any turpentine or cloth…"

"That's not true!" insisted Lisbeth. She crouched and began to collect the bits of dried grass that scattered around during the rope-making process. Then she wrapped the bunch around a branch that hadn't been used for the fire yet. When done, the branch flashed. Lisbeth checked the properties window and then pumped her fist.

"See, dried grass can be flammable, too! The item name is just crude torch, but it'll last longer than the stick by itself."

"Ooh, this is actually very clever for you, Liz!" said Silica, clapping her hands twice and following her lead. When she placed the crude torch into the fire to light it, the effect was much brighter than the branch alone.

"This should really help with gathering the other materials!"

"You bet. Now let's go rustle up some more dried grass and branches!"

With their torches alight, they took a few steps toward the hollow when Lisbeth turned back around.

"Wait, Silica. What did you mean, very clever for me?"

"What a late reaction!" Silica shouted. Yui giggled with delight, and Pina even chirped to join in the fun.

There were no green plants in the wilderness around the cliff hollow, but dried grasses with sharp, jagged edges—the whithergrass in question—and withered trees the color of bone were here and there, so it wasn't that hard to forage for what they needed. Still, the only blade they had was Silica's dagger, so she had to be the one to cut the grass, while Lisbeth focused on whacking off the branches of the dead trees with her mace. Yui offered to carry the torches, but they needed to get her a weapon soon. Only then would they know if an AI could fight as well as a player could.

Silica walked next to Yui with the impromptu torch for a light source, and when she found a whithergrass, she grabbed the whole bundle at the root with her free hand, then sliced through it all with the dagger and tossed the plants into her inventory.

Issreidr, her dagger, was an excellent weapon she acquired in Jotunheim. Originally, it had a bunch of special effects like added ice damage and increased stats and resistances. But looking at the properties now, it only inflicted physical slashing damage, and everything else had vanished. But the damage number itself was far higher than the tree branches, so she had to rely on it for now. If Yui's suspicions about a grace period were correct, however, and it ended, or she removed it from her equipment screen at any point, it would probably be too heavy for a level-1 character to lift again.

The same could be said of Lisbeth's mace, so they wanted to get new weapons not just for Yui, but for themselves as well. However, there were no shops out here in the empty wilderness, and even if there were, they didn't have a single copper coin to their names. At this rate, within a couple of hours, they'd be forced to wear clothes woven of grass and carry wooden clubs like primitive folk.

If it comes to that, I want to make sure Liz dresses down first, so I can get my laughs in, she thought as she chopped off another whithergrass plant.

At that moment, Pina growled deep in its throat, from atop Silica's head. *"Krrruuu..."*

It was a warning. Silica had known her companion for years and could understand the finer nuances of its vocalizations. *Multiple things are approaching from a distance, but I don't know if they're hostile* was the message. Silica's triangular ears swiveled, and she got the feeling that she heard footsteps on the night breeze.

"Put out the torch, Yui!" she said quietly. Yui promptly stuck the flames into the sand. It was immediately dark, but not complete darkness. Lisbeth was still striking a tree less than twenty feet away.

"Liz, something's coming!"

Lisbeth was a blacksmith by trade but an excellent macer in combat, and her reaction was quick. She smacked the torch against the ground to put it out, then rushed back, her steps light and quiet.

"Wolf? Scorpion?" she whispered, but Silica shook her head.

"Pina doesn't know what it is, so it must be neither of those. Something new."

"Probably best not to rush out and attack wildly, then," said the blacksmith. She pointed to a large nearby rock. They moved over to hide behind it, side by side. At this moment, the darkness

of night was welcome. If it was the kind of monster that targeted by sight, it would have a hard time spotting the three of them here.

Silica listened again. She didn't know if the cait sith's listening bonus still worked here, but the footsteps were clearer than before. It seemed to be coming from the northeast direction on the map—the opposite of where New Aincrad landed.

Suddenly, she was aware of a faint vibration. It was Yui, her body pressed against Silica, trembling.

I guess even an AI is frightened in this situation...

Instantly, Silica felt ashamed for thinking that. Yui was an AI, but she could enjoy and take delight in things, as well as feel love, so of course she could have the opposite feelings, too. She'd just been given an HP bar for the first time in her life, and now she was out in the darkness, listening to some unknown thing approaching. Her being afraid was only natural.

And because Yui was helping them with their skill leveling when New Aincrad went down, she'd been separated from Kirito and Asuna. She must have been dying to see her beloved parents again, but rather than logging out, she was staying here with Silica and Lisbeth to help.

She had to protect Yui herself.

With that in mind, she pulled Yui's shoulder closer and whispered, "It's all right. Even in this situation, Liz and I are pretty tough."

"That's right. If anything comes at us, *kapow*! Strike one!" Lisbeth murmured, holding her mace with both hands like a baseball bat.

"Liz, a strike is when..."

...the batter swings and misses, Silica was going to say, but she didn't get to finish. They heard a deep, thick voice from a surprisingly close distance.

Not the growling of a monster. A human voice.

But no matter how hard they listened, the words themselves were unintelligible. It wasn't an issue of volume; the voice was not speaking Japanese—or any other language Silica could recognize.

"𐤔𐤔𐤔𐤔𐤔, 𐤔𐤔𐤔𐤔."

The strange voice was oddly warped, like some kind of magic spell rather than words. It echoed off the rocks behind them. Then another voice responded.

"𐤔𐤔, 𐤔𐤔𐤔𐤔𐤔."

Silica held her breath and clutched Yui's body harder. Lisbeth raised her mace at the ready.

A number of footsteps sounded, sifting the sandy ground. They approached the group from the right, passed just behind the rock—then began to move farther on to the left.

But it was too early to relax. If this was some kind of staged event battle, the footsteps could fade out, then come rushing back, or suddenly jump at them from the opposite direction. If the voices belonged to monsters or NPCs rather than players, the game system would be well aware that the three players were there, after all.

Silica listened to the fading footsteps, being cautious of not just the left side, but the right and above. Once she was sure the figure was far enough away, she finally pulled her back off of the rock and carefully peered around the side.

Three human beings were walking across the wilderness.

They did not appear to be players. All three were men, wearing simple armor made of cloth and leather, carrying large torches in their left hands and spears or axes in their right. Their exposed skin, of which there was a lot, was grayish-brown. Their hair was tied into narrow braids that hung from the top of their heads to nearly the waist.

The trio walked in a straight line, occasionally looking around them. They were heading for the tall cliff that spanned the wilderness from east to west. And as soon as she recognized this, Silica gritted her teeth, realizing their mistake.

A tiny spot at the foot of the cliff was faintly glowing. It was the campfire they had left burning at the hollow.

For an instant, when they were leaving the campfire behind, she had considered putting it out. But it had been a difficult process of striking different kinds of rocks together to spark the fire in the first place, and she didn't want to go through it all over again. Clearly, the men had noticed the light of the fire from a distance and gone to inspect it.

If they put out the fire, that was one thing. But there was also that pile of sixty whithergrass ropes in the hollow with it. If they destroyed or stole those, that would significantly decrease the chances of building a proper shelter before the grace period ended.

"Our ropes," murmured Lisbeth, who was thinking the same thing.

Should they focus on safety and hide here? Or chase after the men for the sake of the ropes? Silica wasn't sure which was the better option.

What would *he* do in this situation? What would the Black Swordsman's choice be?

Give up on the items and stay hidden? No, he wouldn't do that. He might not launch a preemptive attack, but he would at least make contact with them and try to protect what was worth protecting...and he'd find a way to enjoy the situation for what it was.

New Aincrad had fallen, their characters were reset, and the whole game system was different—but it was an undeniable truth that *Unital Ring* was still a game. You could log out, and since they were using AmuSpheres, losing all your HP didn't mean dying. She was level-1 again, but she still had her gear and her Short Sword skill. The proper choice was to act.

"Yui...you stay here," she whispered after three seconds of gathering her courage.

"But—," Yui protested. Silica squeezed her tight, then let go. She made eye contact with Lisbeth, and they were ready to go.

Silica pressed Yui against the side of the rock, then leaped out of the hiding spot and began to sprint. Lisbeth was soon at her side. They'd put their torches out, but the men had light of their own to follow.

After weaving around a rock about Silica's height, they could see the trio. They were already at the entrance to the hollow, peering inside with their weapons raised.

Once they were within ten yards, the men sprang upright.

"אאאאאא‼" shouted the spearman, spinning around. The two axmen took positions to the sides. Based on his equipment and decorations, the one with the spear was their leader. They had fierce war paint on their faces, but even beneath that, it was clear that their expressions were hostile, too.

Silica stopped about fifteen feet away from the men and shouted desperately, "W-we do not wish to fight you!"

She slipped the dagger in her right hand into the sheath behind her back. Lisbeth pointed her mace straight downward and announced, "We just don't want you to take those ropes away from us!"

But their expressions didn't change. One of them inched forward and again shouted, "אאאא‼"

It sounded less like words and more like some kind of totally unintelligible electronic noise. That meant their own speech probably meant nothing to the other side. And these were definitely not players, but NPCs.

"אא…," growled one of the axmen. The tall spearman nodded back. He held out his weapon, its metal tip gleaming and sharp, as he moved closer to the girls. A battle seemed unavoidable.

Silica was preparing for the worst when a voice said, "Keep talking to them a bit longer!"

She gasped. It was Yui, who had left the rock behind and followed them here.

If it turned into a battle with these men, and they lost all their HP, Silica and Lisbeth would either revive somewhere else or, in a worst-case scenario, be cut off from the game. But there was no guarantee it would work the same way for Yui. If it was some kind of error that she'd been turned from a navigation pixie in *ALO* to a player here, there was no telling what might happen if she died. Perhaps it would cause damage to her core program on Kirito's PC...or worse...

They'd have to attack first if they were going to protect Yui, Silica thought. She clenched the hilt of her dagger, but Yui spoke again before she could strike.

"What they're speaking is a variation on the default JA language setting of the Seed format! It's Japanese! There's just a multilayered filter on it. If I have more samples, I might be able to decode it!"

Silica found it difficult to understand what she meant. But she got the general gist of it: The gray-skinned men were actually speaking Japanese—it just didn't sound that way to her.

She threw her hands out and shouted, "Wait! We don't want to fight you!"

Pina picked up on her intent and squeaked "*Kweee!*" from atop her head.

The spearman's eyes passed over Silica's head, and he shouted back, "אאא, אא!"

The axmen at his sides replied, "אאא! אא!" Their hostility did not fade. The pointy end of the spear grew closer and closer. In another three feet, Silica would be within the enemy's striking range.

"...If they start with us, Silica, you pick up Yui and run away," Lisbeth whispered, and Silica nodded back. It would hurt to lose those sixty ropes, but they weren't worth Yui's safety.

I'll wait three seconds, then kick up sand and run for it, Silica thought. She tensed, putting strength in her right foot. *One, two...*

"אאאא, אאאאאא!!" said a voice that did not belong to the three men.

It was Yui. The distorted and noisy affect sounded exactly like the men's voices.

The spearman flinched and leaned away, blinking with shock. His expression of pure hostility shifted into one mixed with confusion and hesitation as he turned to look at his companions.

"…אאאאא?"

Silica couldn't understand anything the man said except that it was a question somehow. Yui answered with something else. Their conversation continued back and forth briefly, and to the girls' disbelief, the men suddenly lowered their weapons and smiled with relief.

Yui came walking up past them, then turned around in front of the girls.

"Silica, Liz, it is safe now. These people are warriors of the Bashin tribe that lives on the highlands north of here. They saw New Aincrad fall and came to investigate what happened. They were afraid we were demons transformed into people, but when I told them that we were simply lost, they believed me."

"…Demons…," Silica mumbled.

Liz shook her head. "I mean, talk about rude. Have you ever seen a demon this cute?"

"You're about as greedy as one."

"Did you say something?"

"Not at all."

While they bickered, the spearman walked into the hollow and pointed at the heap of whithergrass ropes stacked up on the floor. He looked at them and asked, "אאאא, אא?"

"He is asking *Did you make these?*" Yui interpreted. Silica nodded, and the spearman spoke some more.

"He is asking *Do you know the proper way to eat them?*"

"…"

She and Lisbeth shared a look, then shook their heads in unison.

"אאאאא."

"He says: *I will teach you the way if you follow us.*"

"………"

They didn't seem to have the option of refusing. The spearman beckoned them, and the group started walking with the men in the direction they came from.

"…Well, we've passed the plate of no return," said Lisbeth.

"I think you're mixing your metaphors," said Silica, who trotted into the hollow and lifted up the pile of ropes. They'd have to pause their material gathering for now, but at this rate, they might not need to build a shelter after all.

Please let there not be more trouble after this, Silica prayed as she and her friends followed the Bashin warriors to the northeast.

5

Mom's dinner was a brown stew chock-full of mushrooms and chicken. Since it was the first thing I'd asked for after coming home from *SAO*, I considered it my favorite ever since.

I did love it, of course, and sometimes I tried my hand at making it. But I couldn't bring myself to be honest and admit to my mom that the reason I loved it was deeply tied to memories within Aincrad, and that it was originally a rabbit stew, rather than chicken.

In fact, all my favorite dishes—teri-mayo burgers, salt-flavored ramen, and honey pies—came from virtual-world memories. If those memories from the past faded, I might no longer want to eat those foods, but for the moment, that didn't seem likely.

I sent one e-mail before eating, then took off my Augma so I could enjoy my meal—despite working with tech as the editor in chief of an IT magazine, Mom was very picky about device manners at the table. When I had put all the dishes away, the living room clock said it was 7:22. Only three minutes until I was supposed to meet back up with Asuna. Mom was enjoying her post-dinner coffee on the sofa; I thanked her for the meal and headed back upstairs. Suguha followed behind me and said "I'm going to take a bath, okay?" before heading toward her room. I yanked on the back of her collar.

"*Gweh*...Wh-what was that for?!"

"We need to talk. It's important. Bring your AmuSphere over to my room right now."

"H...huh?"

I can't say I didn't deserve the suspicious look she gave me. Regardless, I grabbed my sister's shoulders, spun her around, and pushed her forward. "On the double!" Suguha went into her room grumbling, but she came back out with her AmuSphere in one hand and her phone in the other. I beckoned her in.

Once she was inside my room, I shut the door and asked her as quickly as I could, "Sugu, where's your resurrect point right now?!"

"Huh...? It's in your house...on the twenty-second floor of New Aincrad."

"Good. And that's the last place where you logged out?"

"That's right. What is this all about?"

"I'll explain inside. Get ready to dive."

"Dive...from here?!" she said, her eyes wide as she looked around my room. "But you don't even have any cushions in here. Am I supposed to just lie on the floor?"

"We can each take half the bed. C'mon, hurry!"

I pushed her shoulders again and sat her on the bed. She looked up at me, her mouth working silently. I plucked the AmuSphere from her hands and plopped it onto her head.

"Ah, h-hey, wait..."

Just then, the phone in Suguha's hand beeped with a notification. She looked at the screen reflexively, and her thick eyebrows lowered. "Oh, it's from Nagata...Yikes! Look at all the e-mails and calls!"

"Ignore them. I know what he wants," I said mercilessly, causing Suguha's mouth to drop open again.

"H...huh...?"

"There's something more important to deal with now. C'mon, take the other side."

"Sheesh…" Suguha pouted but placed her phone on the headboard, then went to lie down on the back side of the bed. I positioned myself next to her and put on my AmuSphere, lowered the visor, and glanced at the clock in the lower left of the interior monitor as I waited for it to boot up. It was 7:24:47.

There wasn't really a need to hit the timing on the exact second, but I took a deep breath anyway and said, "We'll dive on a countdown of five, four, three, two, one…"

"Link Start!"

When gravity kicked in and sank the soles of my shoes against hard floor again, I opened my eyes to see that the undine in the white knight uniform and the cait sith wearing golden armor were already waiting in the log cabin's living room. It was dark inside, lit only by the weak handmade torch stuck into the crack in the wall.

Asuna and Alice were about to say something when they saw me, but then their eyes moved to my right. Two seconds later, a fourth figure appeared beside me, and they cried out.

"It's Leafa!"

"Leafa!"

They rushed over and clutched the arms of the sylph magic warrior.

"You're all right! I'm so glad…"

"We were really worried!"

Suguha, now in character as Leafa, looked absolutely perplexed. She stared at the two of them.

"Um, Asuna, Alice…what do you mean, all right…? Why is it so dark in here?"

Then she looked at me, and her jaw dropped once again.

"B-Big Brother…why are you dressed like that?!"

"I'm going to need you to overlook my state of dress for now," I said, glancing down at my underwear-clad avatar briefly before looking up at my sister. The lightweight green armor and long katana she kept at her left hip belonged to her usual battle outfit. She didn't seem encumbered by it. That meant the grace period for carrying equipment weight was still active. Leafa's ears had become more human-shaped, but it was such a subtle change that even she hadn't noticed yet.

Relieved, I asked her, "Sugu...I mean, Leafa, was anything different about the *ALO* login sequence?"

"Huh? Oh...yeah, I was a bit confused during the falling sequence...I passed straight through some patterned wheel thing. That was different than usual. What was it?"

"...I knew it...," I murmured. I'd seen that image once before. It was when I had converted my spriggan avatar into the shooting-centric world of *Gun Gale Online*.

"That's the converting ring. When you logged in, your avatar was forcibly converted into this world's style."

"H-huh?! Converted...? But this is your usual home, Big Br...I mean, it's Kirito and Asuna's home...," Leafa said, looking around the darkened living room.

Then she pressed her hands to her mouth and uttered hoarsely, "Wh...what the...? Asuna, what happened?!"

I couldn't blame her for being shocked. All the interior objects, the furniture and decorations that Asuna had put so much work into selecting and arranging, were gone from the spacious living room.

And that wasn't all. The back wall where there had once been a large fireplace was utterly shattered, exposing the outdoors. The center of the floor was severely dented. There were holes in the ceiling here and there. I'd seen the damage many times by now, but it still made my heart hurt.

Asuna moved her hand from Leafa's arm to her back and said, "Leafa, we're not in Alfheim anymore. We were teleported into this world with our cabin...well, no, I suppose with all of New Aincrad."

*   *   *

We sat in a circle in the spot where the big, puffy couch had once been and imparted our current knowledge to Leafa.

She listened, hugging her knees, and nodded when we were done, her long golden ponytail swaying. She glanced sidelong at me.

"I see...Now I get why you're dressed like that."

"Your understanding means the world to me. Asuna and Alice still have their armor, but they can't equip their swords anymore...so yours is all we can count on right now, Leafa."

"...So you brought me here to be your bodyguard?"

"Well, uh, not *only* that," I said hastily.

My sister glared at me, then looked out at the forest through the collapsed wall. "What kind of monsters show up around here?"

"We still haven't seen any creatures yet," answered Alice. She reached for her empty sword belt on instinct. It was a lonely gesture. "But when we went into the forest to look for kindling earlier, there were multiple howls in the distance. It seems certain that something is living in this forest."

"Ugh...and if I'm level-1, then I can't use magic..."

"Yes, the sacred arts...er, the spells used in Alfheim did not have any effect here. If Yui were here, she might be able to explain things to us. Were you able to communicate with her on the other side, Kirito?"

Even in the dark, Alice's blue eyes shone as bright as sapphires. I stared back into them and said, "No, she didn't respond. I think she's probably still here somewhere with Liz and Silica."

"Hmm...I hope we can regroup with them. If they were inside New Aincrad, then they can't be too far away..."

"Oh, about that!" Leafa said, leaning forward. "I get that New Aincrad fell down to earth, but what happened after that? Did you see everything, Kirito?"

"We were so desperate to give this cabin a softer landing that I didn't have time to watch it..."

"Besides, Leafa," said Asuna, putting her hands in the air to explain, "the piece of rock that split off kind of rode across the air with us on it, at a thirty-degree angle or so…If New Aincrad fell from a height of six miles, then our landing point would be about ten and a half miles away. There were some rocky mountains below us at points, so the truth is, we didn't even hear the sound of New Aincrad crashing to the ground."

"Ten miles…That would be an easy trip if we had wings," Leafa lamented, wriggling her back, but of course, no fairy wings appeared. She was so enamored with flying that she had the nickname Speedaholic. Losing them had to be an even bigger shock than having her character stats reset.

But true to her nature, my sister put on a brave smile and took it in stride.

"All right, I have a grasp of the situation. So your goal for now is to repair this house, right? Then I'll help, of course! This is *my* home, too!"

"…Thank you, Leafa," Asuna said, momentarily surprised. She squeezed my sister's hands kindly and turned her gaze to the damaged living room. "Calculating from the rate of durability decrease, we've got a bit over ten hours until the building is destroyed…and we still have a bunch of materials to gather by then. What we need are…"

Asuna tapped the floor to bring up the properties window of the house and showed Leafa the screen of items needed to conduct the repair process. While they talked this over, I opened my ring menu and chose the SKILLS icon.

The window that appeared contained a list of skills I'd gained. At the top was the One-Handed Sword skill that was a holdover from *ALO*, but it was useless at the moment, since I couldn't use my actual sword.

Below that was a list of crafting and support skills I'd learned since we landed here. Stoneworking, Woodworking, Weaving, and Physique. All of them were barely more than zero, but they were my lifeline for the moment.

I tapped the Stoneworking skill, and a new window appeared displaying my current proficiency and the items I could craft with it. Among the primitive weapons like stone knife, stone ax, and stone spear was a stone sword. If it came to it, that was going to have to be my weapon, but it was all too easy to imagine Suguha rolling around and crying with laughter when she saw me holding a stone sword in my undies, so I was hoping to make my first weapon a metal one.

Next to the names of the stone weapons was a hammer symbol. Curious, I tapped it, and a smaller pop-up that said *Tips* materialized with a little jingle.

Items displayed with this icon must be created manually, by hand or with a tool.

That would suggest that some items *didn't* need to be created that way, so I scrolled farther through the list. After the weapons were tools like stone plates, stone hammers, and whetstones, followed by building materials like stone blocks and stone foundations. All the items so far had the manual symbol next to them.

At the very bottom were names like stone hut and stone hearth and stone furnace, and they had a symbol that looked like two overlapping rectangles next to them. I tapped that icon, and the pop-up jingled again.

Items displayed with this icon can be produced from the skill window. All the necessary materials must be in your inventory already.

"I see…"

I tapped the stone hut to bring up the list of needed materials. There was a PRODUCE button at the bottom of the window. Out of sheer momentum, I pressed it, but of course, it said *You do not have the necessary materials.*

"Ooh, there's a furnace for smelting iron!" exclaimed Alice, who came over to look at my window. "Couldn't we use that to create the iron sheets and nails and such to repair the log cabin? As well as make new weapons?"

"Well, I suppose that's right," I said, unable to commit to a positive or negative answer. "But we'll need iron ore to make iron, of course, and it's not that easy to find in games like this. I doubt we'll find it just growing out of the ground in the middle of the plains."

"Where do you acquire it, then?"

"The orthodox way is on a mountain or in a cave. But there aren't any mountains around here…"

"Which leaves a cave," said the cat-eared knight. She did not sound enthused.

Something I learned since we started adventuring together in *ALO* was that the bold and seemingly flawless knight I met in the Underworld actually did have a natural weakness to some things. One was natural caves; while she was perfectly comfortable in human-constructed dungeons and catacombs, she did not like to go into caves and grottoes formed by natural forces. I suspected it had to do with some distant childhood memories that were supposedly deleted, but I'd never considered it important enough to ask her about.

"Well, I doubt we'll just happen across caves wherever we wander…so let's focus on wrapping up all the materials we can make with wood first. Especially now that we have our helpful lumberjack with us."

Leafa spun around, incensed. "Excuse me, Kirito! Are you referring to me?! All I have is this sword!"

"And it'll do. When I was in the Underworld, I cut down a tree that couldn't be cut down for a thousand years, and that was with a single longswo—"

"Okay, okay, I'll do it," she interrupted so that she wouldn't have to listen to me brag. "But based on what you said, my ability to use this sword will only last during the…what did you call it? Grace period? How many more hours is that?"

"Um, to find that out, we'd have to ask the person behind this whole state of affai—," I said, until Alice jabbed me in the side. "*Gah!* Wh…what was that for?"

"Here, Kirito, look at this," she said, ignoring my protest and opening her ring menu. I stared at them, but the eight purple icons seemed no different from my own.

"...What am I looking at?"

"The color of the icons. Does it seem like the coloring shifts as they rotate right?"

"Oh...that's true!" shouted Asuna. She'd opened her own menu and was nodding as she examined it. "Yes, the icon at the very top is more reddish, but as you go clockwise, they get bluer and bluer, until the eighth one is like a bluish-purple. But...what is it about that, Alice?"

"When I looked at this right after landing, I recall that nearly all the icons were tinted blue. It imprinted in my mind because I thought they looked like the shade of zephilia flowers. But right now, their colors are changing, up to about the fifth icon...Could this be depicting the amount of time left in the grace period?"

"Ohhh...I see what you mean..."

I closed all the crafting windows and stared at the base menu. If they represented a kind of timer, like Alice said...then about five icons had changed color in two and a half hours. Thirty minutes for each one.

"...If there are only three icons left, that gives an hour and a half until they all have changed color..."

"What...? That's it?!" exclaimed Leafa, looking around the room as if searching for a wall clock.

Alice closed her ring menu and said tersely, "Let's hurry. We should at least cut down all the trees we need while we can still use Leafa's sword."

Leafa didn't complain this time. She gripped the sheath of her long katana and said seriously, "All right. I'll chop down the trees. You strip off the bark."

"We know what to do. So let's get busy, Leafa," said Asuna. With that, we rushed out of the open doorway.

But we stopped before we even got off the brutalized porch. The overwhelming darkness of the forest at night seemed to consume us. Even outside, we couldn't see more than a dozen feet or so ahead of us.

"...I think we're going to need light...," I murmured, and the surroundings grew a tiny bit brighter. Not because the game itself was being helpful, but because Alice brought out the impromptu torch we were using to light the cabin.

"How did you make the sparks to light that, by the way?" I asked belatedly.

Alice pulled two egg-sized rocks from the pouch she had on her belt to show me. "I returned a bit before you two did, so I looked for flint rocks at the river. I thought we'd need them when it got dark."

"N-nice one..."

I should have figured that someone actually from another world would have her head on straight!

"So how do you use them?"

"It's actually easier here than it is in the Underworld. You just bunch up the dead grass into tinder, then strike the sparks about ten times until it catches. Then you transfer the fire to the branch."

"Hmm..."

I prefer the magic way! I moaned inwardly but managed to hold my silence. In *SAO*, where there was no magic, we usually had lanterns, but given that you lit those by simply tapping them, that was essentially magic, too. The world of *Unital Ring* was not going to make things easy for us.

"Well, I'll go look for more..."

But before I could even finish my sentence, Alice hopped down to the ground, took a few steps, then crouched. There was a large selection of dead branches there that I hadn't seen before. She extended the torch into its midst, and they soon began to snap and pop with great force.

"Oh wow! The fire effects are so realistic!" Leafa exclaimed. I couldn't blame her. The dancing red flames and soaring sparks were so fine in their detail that I couldn't tell the difference from a real campfire. As I thought when I first saw the trees in the forest, the graphical quality of this world was far beyond that of *ALO*...and even *SAO*. In terms of the visual impact, it was like upgrading a flat-panel display from HD quality to 4K.

But it was also something that didn't add up with the information I'd collected when I logged out.

It wasn't just us *ALO* players who'd gotten converted here against our will. It was the majority of the major VRMMOs that made up The Seed Nexus. Probably hundreds of thousands of players from over a hundred virtual worlds in all. Did the system capacity exist in 2026 to have a world large enough to hold so many players and yet contain so much incredible detail...?

"Kirito, wake up and help out!"

A hand slapped my bare back, and I jumped. "Yeow!"

"You're the one who said we didn't have time. Let's get moving!"

"R-right..."

Like Leafa said, this was the time for action, not reflection. Alice's campfire was burning vigorously now, casting reddish light on the forest surrounding the clearing. We could do plenty of work like this without needing to carry torches.

"Okay, let's do this...," I started to say.

But Leafa already had her blade out, swinging it fiercely at the nearest spiral pine. *Shwack!* It made a nice, pleasing sound. Meanwhile, I was standing there with my fist raised at an awkward height, earning me mixed glances from Asuna and Alice.

After we save our house, I'm going to get myself some new gear, I swore to myself. *Even if it means going to school after an all-nighter.*

True to its nature as an Ancient weapon in *ALO*, Leafa's sword sliced up the spiral pines like they were nothing, despite not being a proper woodcutting ax. It took no more than thirty seconds for her to cut down a tree, so even with three people working on skinning and hauling it off, any delay would cause our side of the process to get backed up.

After fifteen minutes of high-focus teamwork with Asuna and Alice, we had another tremendous stack of spiral-patterned logs in the clearing. There were three piles of ten logs each. That should be more than enough to make the seventy-five sawed planks we needed for the repair.

But as I stood there satisfied, hands on my hips, a question occurred to me.

"Um…how do we make the planks…?"

There were plenty of planks available for purchase at the local home improvement store in the real world, but I didn't know exactly how they made them. I guessed they probably just sliced the logs into thinner pieces…but you'd probably need some heavy-duty equipment to process logs of this width.

Asuna had the knowledge to back up my guess. "Of course, we don't have a large band saw here, so we'll at least need a frame saw…"

"F-frame saw?"

"Yes, it's a huge saw they used back in the Meiji era."

"Ohhh…I think maybe I've seen that in a Japanese history textbook once…"

I'd never heard of a band saw, either, but I could guess that it was the name of another kind of wood-processing tool. "So we need a saw…We might be able to craft one with iron and the Blacksmithing skill, but both of those will probably take a lot of time. But then again…they didn't have saws all the way back in the earliest periods of Japanese history, right? So how did those people make planks of wood?"

"Well, let's see…"

Even brilliant Asuna had to pause and make a face like she was searching her memory, but as always, she found the answer there. That's how I could tell her brain was simply different from mine.

"A saw that can cut a log vertically, like the frame saw I mentioned…came to Japan from the Asian mainland in the fourteenth or fifteenth century. Before that, they would hammer wedges into the logs to split them, then use hand axes and planes to finish the surfaces. Splitting wood with a wedge is basically just hoping the grain will split in your favor, so it was inefficient and susceptible to failure. Longer planks were a real extravagance back in those days."

"Huh…With wedges, eh?" I murmured, gazing at the stacks of logs.

I'd been examining them as we stripped the bark off. The name spiral pine definitely referred to the way the tree rotated like a drill as it grew. The fibers were twisted into a spiral pattern inside the trunk. If this game could even factor in grain direction to individual trees, then striking them with wedges was almost certainly going to shatter them without a straight split. And we couldn't get a wedge either until our little civilization in the forest clearing reached the Iron Age.

"Rrrmmm…wood planks really are a product of humanity's wisdom," I said, impressed.

Asuna said, "That's true, but that's not all. You can only get a proper plank from the center of a log, so it's really the life and history of a tree that's lived for decades. I feel like if you consider it from that angle, it only makes sense that it's difficult to create planks from trees."

"That's true. And yet, somehow, we have to make this into a plank, or we can't repair our cabin…," I said, slapping the end of the log.

Just then, Leafa came back from her task with Alice and smacked me hard on the back.

"Yeow!"

"Now, now, Kirito. You'd better not be discounting my skill and the power of Lysavindr here."

"Ouch…why does everyone keep slapping me on the back…?"

"Ha-ha-ha! When you look like that, it's impossible to resist. Wanna give him a whack, Asuna?"

"You could pick a better way of saying that!" I protested, leaping away from them. I thought Asuna looked momentarily disappointed, but I hoped it was a trick of the light. Either way, I had to be more careful to keep my back pointed away from these women.

"A-anyway," I said to Leafa, "what was that about your skill?"

"Just move out of the way."

She gestured for the rest of us to back away, then stood in front of the pile of logs. Her silver blade was perfectly still in her hands, resting in an orthodox forward stance.

"Um, Sugu, you aren't going to chop those logs with your sword, are you—?" I asked, accidentally using her real name.

Without turning away, the sylph warrior said, "I've cut down thirty of them, so I think I've got the hang of it now. Just watch."

At that point, I had no choice. The flat of Lysavindr gleamed red with the reflected light of the campfire.

Categorically speaking, Leafa's long katana was considered a bastard sword, meaning that when wielded in one hand, she could use One-Handed Sword skills, and when held with both, she could use Two-Handed Sword skills. There was a downside that came with that convenience, though; it was heavy and difficult to use with one hand but lighter and less powerful than a proper two-handed sword. But as a kendo athlete, she claimed that it was just the right length and weight.

As the rest of us watched, Leafa lifted her blade as smoothly as though drawn by invisible strings. Then she paused and held it for just a moment so that a green glow infused it—the visual effect that indicated an imminent sword skill. I was already certain because weapon skills still existed, but this was further confirmation that the numerous special attacks from the original *SAO* were still carried over into this game.

"...*Haah!*" Leafa barked, swinging her sword. Two slices split the night air: the two-part Two-Handed Sword skill Cataract.

Normally, it was consecutive high swings that went *wham, wham!* But Leafa's version was so fast that they both seemed to happen in a single breath. The slashes entered the edge of the log on top of the pile, the green light passing all the way through to the other end before vanishing.

After a second's pause, the log silently split into two, then tumbled to the ground. In the center, between the spot where the two slashes had gone, was a single, thin plank of wood. It, too, toppled over to the right and would have fallen to the ground if I hadn't leaped forward to snatch it first.

It was about three-quarters of an inch thick. The surface was as smooth as if it had been lovingly planed, and the grain was vivid and diagonal. I tapped it with my left hand to bring up the properties window. It was called a sawed aged spiral pine plank.

"What do you think, Kirito? Will that work for repairing the cabin?" asked my sister as she lowered her sword. I gave her a thumbs-up.

"It's perfect. But..."

I put the freshly cut plank into my inventory, then glanced at the two parts of the vertically split log on the ground.

"...This method can only make one plank per log...We need to create some means of supporting the logs first..."

"Huh? Just use your hands," she said breezily. Then she pointed at one of the log's split halves and said, "Put that back up on the pile, then hold it up vertically."

"......"

I had a bad feeling about this, but I did as she said, picking it up and placing it back where it was before—but standing on the point of its severed edge. Once it was balanced just right, I used both hands to hold it up.

"Now hold it *right there*. Here goes..."

Leafa raised her sword again and easily activated a sword skill. This was the simple one-hit Two-Handed Sword skill Cascade. The blade hit three-quarters of an inch from the previous cut, the green light flashing through the bottom of my hand.

"Yikes!" I yelped. There was a light shock from the effect, but no damage. I would have let go, except that Leafa instructed, "Hold it right there!"

This time, she used Cataract again, which had just finished its cooldown. Then Cascade once more, followed by Cataract.

After six slashes in total, the object itself must have run out of durability, because the end of the log shattered like glass. I was left with six long slabs of wood, perfectly parallel, if slightly varied in size—this was unavoidable, because a log is a round cylinder. Added to the initial plank, this meant we'd gotten seven planks of wood from the half-split log.

"Brilliant work, Leafa!" marveled Alice, who gave her a little round of applause. "When I was living in seclusion near Rulid, I made a living by felling trees, but I was never able to carve them into planks so skillfully."

"Teh-heh-heh-heh, aw, it's nothing." Leafa chuckled rather creepily.

"No, it really is amazing," added Asuna. "Two-Handed Sword skills are tough to control, but you landed them with perfect accuracy. I don't even think Kirito can do that."

What?! I balked. But I had no way of demonstrating my incredible skill at this moment. Instead, I silently put the six planks in my inventory, circled around the other side of the stack, and lifted the other half of the log into place.

"Let's keep this up and get through the rest of the logs, dear sister," I instructed.

Leafa happily cried "You got it!" and raised her sword again.

When she was done slicing through the ten logs, it was after eight o'clock. There was a little less than an hour until the grace period on our equipment weight ended.

Because Leafa's log-splitting exhibition almost never missed, we'd gained 130 planks, but overall, we'd still only filled out two of the six types of materials needed to repair our log cabin. And the other four would be difficult to acquire. We didn't even know how to get them.

"Now we have to do something about iron," muttered Asuna, staring into the weakening light of the campfire.

I folded my arms and said, "Yes...I should be able to make a furnace with stones from the riverbed, but that doesn't solve the matter of the ore to put inside it. I'm sure we'll find some in a cave, like we talked about earlier, but there are bound to be monsters...and tougher ones than what we'll find outside..."

"I know...If we could just use our swords...," Asuna lamented, looking at her hand. I felt the same way—in fact, I was doubly frustrated because I couldn't wear armor, either. Giving us four hours of time to ignore that rule was fine and dandy, but converting everyone's characters by force and telling them *too bad* if you weren't equipping your gear, or took it off for a moment, was just plain cruel. It was common for people to unequip weapons in town or indoors, and there had to be a high percentage of the hundreds of thousands of players dragged into this like Asuna and me, who weren't built to play the tank role and could no longer hold their weapons.

By this point, MMO Today's message boards and various social networks would be bustling with discussion of this incident. I wanted to log out and gather as much information as I could, but the materials to repair the log cabin took precedence. Leafa was our lifeline of hope, and she could only use Lysavindr for a bit longer.

"I have to wonder," Asuna suddenly murmured, "how did you know that my brother had that online connection, Kirito?"

"Er, w-well..."

The very person I sent an e-mail to with my Augma after logging out earlier was Asuna's brother, Kouichirou Yuuki. I knew that he'd installed a secret dedicated line that didn't run through the home server, and I asked him to let Asuna use it. But I didn't have time to explain how I knew about that, so I had to keep it as brief as possible.

"I made Kouichirou a promise to show him around New Aincrad, and that's when I heard about the independent line."

Asuna made a weird kind of gasping noise.

"Wh-what was that?"

"Sorry…it's just that I can't get used to you calling my big brother by his first name. You know how informal that is…"

"Hey, he insisted. At any rate, it means you can dive as late as you want without worrying about being yelled at."

"I feel a bit guilty, but Mama likes this cabin, too, so I feel like I should explain it to him someday," Asuna said, sighing a little bit. Then the moment passed, and she said, "Well, we should head off to find that iron o—"

She didn't finish. There was another wild animal call from the forest. This time, it wasn't distant howling, but clear, hostile growling. It was accompanied by the crackling of twigs and bushes.

"Kirito!" "Big Brother!"

Alice and Leafa rushed over into formation. All four of us readied our weapons, but only Leafa had a proper sword. The three indigenous members of the party had only sad, crude stone knives. Still, it was better than nothing, I told myself, squeezing the grip wrapped in grass rope.

Something growled again, closer this time. It was deep and guttural, *brrrrr*, like the idling sound of a large motorcycle. Obviously, there wouldn't be anything like that in this world. I squinted into the dark woods, but the brightness of our campfire left me unable to see anything beyond the first few rows of trees.

*Perhaps we should put out the fire…*But if these were animal-type monsters, they might be afraid of flames. I had to assume that if we put it out, there would be no way to relight the kindling with the inefficient method of striking up sparks once we were in the midst of battle.

As if to punctuate my hesitation, a third short growl sounded. The cracking sound of twigs being stepped on approached slowly from the north of the clearing toward the west. The owner of that voice was just beyond the tree line.

"We'll be fine," I said in a voice hoarse enough to indicate that we were not fine. "It might be a monster, but I'm sure it's just a wimpy starter monster. Stone knives should be more than enough to kill it."

"...You mean like the blue boars in *SAO*?" Asuna asked.

I nodded. "Yes, something even lower than a boar, like a wolf or a fox or a nutria..."

"Kirito, what is a nutria?" asked Alice. I was about to tell her that it was like a capybara, but then I realized she wouldn't know what a capybara was, either. What were those big rats with the long ears from the Underworld called again...? Before I could recall the answer, an especially ferocious howl came from the woods on the other side of the campfire.

"Grroarrroooo!"

With a tremendous cracking, an entire clump of bushes was flattened, and a huge shadow leaped into the clearing. It charged toward us, shaking the earth, and stood up just before the fire.

It was enormous. Its head was well over six feet off the ground. Its limbs were thick, its head was round, and its claws and fangs were abnormally long and sharp. Its blackish-brown fur was long and shaggy. It was clearly not a wolf or a fox—and definitely not a nutria...

"A b-b-beaaaar!" screamed Leafa, pointing at the creature. Then she swiveled to point at *me*. "You said it was going to be a wimpy one!"

"Huh? That's weird...," I muttered. Then it hit me.

We split off from New Aincrad with the log cabin. Thanks to the air resistance, and possibly the rotational power of the floating castle, we landed over ten miles away. In real-life terms, that was only the distance from my hometown of Kawagoe to the nearby city of Wakoshi, but in RPG terms, it was an endless trek. On top of that, there was no guarantee that New Aincrad's landing point was the "starting zone" for this game. The whole area around us could be full of mid-level monsters instead.

"*Grrrlg...,*" growled the bear, standing on its back legs. The light of the fire clearly illuminated the jagged lightning bolts of white fur under its neck. I supposed that rather than being a moon bear, this was a lightning bear. I wanted to know its official name, but even though it was clearly hostile, the game was not displaying a cursor over the bear's head yet.

Fight or run?

My brain ran on overdrive as I stared at the bear's baleful red eyes. We were all level-1. If the bear was level-10 or so, we stood no chance. But if we ran, our only options were inside the cabin or toward the river to the southwest. There was a huge hole in the cabin wall, and there could be other monsters at the river. Plus, if we ran in the dark without a light, I was sure I'd trip on something and fall in no time.

Just then, there was a loud crunch, and the logs in the fire collapsed, sending up a huge curtain of sparks. On that signal, the bear lowered its front legs to the ground, scratched the dirt with its fierce claws several times, and started to charge.

"We have to fight, Kirito!" yelled Leafa, brandishing her sword.

There was no time to think anymore. I shouted "Take the front!" and leaped to the right of the bear, readying my knife. Asuna jumped to the left, while Alice rushed to help Leafa.

"*Gwoaaah!*" bellowed the bear as it ran. It leaped over the fire, totally unafraid, and landed in front of Leafa. Then it stood on its rear legs again, raising its paws high. Leafa was not a small target by any means, but because the dark pelt of the bear melted into the darkness, it seemed three times bigger than her.

The sylph warrior was not afraid, however.

"*Haah!*" she cried, charging, her long blade flashing right for the bear's exposed left flank. Bright-red damage effects spilled forth, and at last, a red cursor and HP bar appeared over the bear's head.

This was my first glance at a cursor in this game. It took the form of a rotating ring intersected by sharp spindles. The ring featured an HP bar and the monster's name on the top and bottom. It displayed the bear's name in Japanese, rather than the English alphabet, reading *Thornspike Cave Bear.*

I barely had time to process this visual information when four huge claws slashed through my vision. The bear's massive right paw did not connect, however. The loss of Leafa's wings had done nothing to diminish her agility; she nimbly dodged out of the way of the creature's claws and jabbed with her sword again. It was another clean hit...but the bear's HP bar was only down about 10 percent so far.

Lysavindr was one of the greatest of the Ancient weapons in *ALO*, and if its specs carried over to this game, then, even in the hands of a level-1 player, it ought to destroy a starter monster in a single hit. If it was this difficult to do any real damage to it, then the bear had to be an extremely high-ranked monster.

"*Groaaaah!*" it howled with fury, stretching out its arms and trying to block Leafa from escaping. Once it caught her, it likely intended to bite her. She had to be very careful with how she approached it.

But this was the moment that Asuna, who had circled around the bear's rear, bravely made a charge.

"*Yaaaa!*" she shrieked, and immediately after came a heavy thud. The stone knife in her hand sank deep into the bear's fur, and it spilled red light when she promptly pulled it back out.

The damage was minuscule, but it succeeded at drawing the bear's attention. It turned to chase after Asuna, but the rotation was slow, and its feet weren't made for nimble pivoting.

As soon as I sensed the bear's attention was broken, I made

eye contact with Alice, and we leaped into motion together. Without a word, we drove our knives into the beast's flank and back.

"*Goaaah!*" it roared, throwing its head back in pain.

As soon as we leaped out of the way, Leafa activated the One-Handed Sword skill Vertical Arc. It carved a blue *V* into the bear's massive back. This time, it had a visible effect on the HP bar. Now it was down to 70 percent.

We can do this!

With the three knives darting in and out to confuse the bear while Leafa struck it with major attacks, we could finish this in another four—no, three rounds, I felt sure. I breathed in to instruct the group to keep repeating this pattern. Except...

"*Grraaagh!!*" the bear howled, returning its front legs to the ground and jumping toward the forest. Was it going to run away—?

Sadly, that was not the case. It used all four legs to quickly distance itself from us, then whipped around with a cloud of dust and stood up again. It stretched out its arms, pointed its head to the heavens, and arched its huge back as far as it could go.

The very clear lightning-shaped outlines of white fur on its chest suddenly trembled, like they were completely different and distinct animals from the bear.

Something's coming.

I felt a cold shiver down my back and tried to shout "Get out of the..."

But it was too late. The white bristled hair in the lightning patterns stood up like porcupine quills and shot whistling from its chest. There were dozens...hundreds of them.

"Kirito!" Alice shouted. She leaped in front of me and crossed her arms.

We were enveloped in a storm of quills. *Ta-ta-ta-tang!* Metal armor deflected the barbs, while they sank through leather and cloth—and flesh.

In my right shoulder and left leg, I felt not pain, but something very close to it—a mixture of intense heat and cold mixed together.

The HP bar in the upper left corner of my vision lost over 70 percent of its value at once, turning deep orange. The HP of the other three went down, too. I looked at my shoulder and saw a milky-white quill with a metallic sheen stuck in deep, about six inches long and a fraction of an inch wide.

Just two of these took out nearly three-quarters of my health?! I fumed. But I was a level-1 player with no armor, and this monster had to be at least level-10, so I supposed it was a miracle I'd survived at all. And without Alice's protection, I absolutely *would* have died.

Having just demonstrated why it was called a thornspike cave bear, the beast lowered its front paws to the ground and growled in satisfaction, certain of its victory. The fur quills had shot out in quite a spray; there were at least a dozen in Leafa's and Asuna's armor, too. We'd get wiped out if it attacked like that again.

"Let's back away!" I suggested.

But with her stone knife pointed at the bear, Asuna shouted back, "Where will we go?!"

"It has to be inside the cabin!"

"There's no wall!"

Yes, the left wall of the log cabin was damaged to the point that there was a huge, gaping hole there. If the bear got inside…

"We'll just have to deal with it!" I replied. Asuna, Alice, and Leafa all gave me a look that said *I should have known*, but they went along with the plan anyway.

The bear resumed its approach. Its glowing-red eyes were full of menace, warning that if its prey were to turn around and run, it was ready to leap on our backs.

I waved at the other three to back away, while moving steadily away to the right. My destination was the other side of the pile of logs we didn't use for planks. Retreating carefully, so as not to

expose an opening to attack, I waited until the logs blocked the bear's line of sight, then shouted, "Run!"

We sprinted for the entrance to the log cabin, right as the bear roared behind us.

"Gwaooooh!!"

I could feel the vibration of its tremendous weight galloping for us, followed by a cacophonous clattering.

I spun around to see that the bear had charged headfirst through the mound of logs and gotten stuck beneath them when they collapsed. In vain, I hoped it would simply die from the pressure, but of course, we weren't that lucky. The bear easily kicked the tree trunks off and resumed its charge. Its HP bar had gone down a tiny bit, but it still wasn't even halfway done.

"Hurry, Kirito!" Asuna urged. I turned back to see that the women had reached the entryway at the porch. I raced for all I was worth, leaping up the collapsed stairs and into the cabin, grabbing the doorknob and smashing it closed behind me out of sheer momentum.

Thwaaam! A tremendous shock slammed into the door two seconds later, rattling the entire cabin. Bits of dust and wood sprinkled down from the cracked beams and punctured roof.

"H-help prop up the door!" I shouted, but the others were already there, pressing against it. There was another shock. The door twisted more, to the point where I was afraid it would soon pop out of the frame.

After two body blows against the door, I sensed the bear walking away. *Please, let it return to the forest,* I prayed as the footsteps continued to the right.

I moved about on tiptoe, peering outside through the window-sill of broken glass. Instantly, as though waiting for me, the bear bellowed *"Grrfh!"* and charged at us. I panicked and pulled my head back. The bear head-butted the wall anyway. The log wall, which was much stronger than the door, creaked and cracked, and more wood chips fell throughout the living room.

Asuna tapped the nearby wall to take a glance at the properties window and let out a little shriek. "Kirito, the house's durability is going down!"

"Damn…"

I gnashed my teeth, but it was no surprise, after taking three hits from such a huge and powerful body. If we stayed in here, and the bear continued, it would completely knock down the cabin at some point.

There had to be something—some other way to drive the beast off.

I glanced around the room in a desperate haze. If I had that bottle of dried chili peppers in the pantry, I could attack the bear's nose with it, but everything from furniture to food ingredients had been spirited away when we teleported into this world. The only thing left behind was our home storage box, but that was also…

Not empty.

Inspiration struck. I glanced at the box, then at the huge hole in the ceiling, then at the box again. It was very close…but if the range for a trade request here was the same as in *SAO* and *ALO*, it should be just enough.

"Alice, kneel down right there!" I said. The cat-eared knight looked very confused. Then a fourth impact shook the cabin. We didn't have a moment to waste.

Looking grave, Alice did as she was told and knelt down at the spot indicated.

"Sorry about this!" I shouted, placing my bare foot on the right shoulder plate of her armor. Alice squawked in surprise, but I launched myself off of her, stretching as far as my arms could reach.

Even with my reset character stats, I was just barely able to catch the beam with my fingertips. Struggling and rocking my body, I managed to pull myself up, then gave a new order.

"Asuna, pull all the logs out of the home's storage menu and trade them to Leafa!"

After years of working with me, Asuna was used to my baffling and unexplained ideas. Without asking why, she immediately tapped the storage box. After hitting a few buttons on the window, she promptly put her hand down against the floor, as if resisting some terrible invisible weight. But with great determination, she called up the ring menu and sent a trade request to Leafa, who was waiting about six feet away.

Once the source of all that encumbrance moved, it was Leafa's turn to fall to her knees. "It's so heavyyyy!" she groaned. Before I could even tell her what to do, she was busy getting it done; she sent a trade window to Alice, who accepted the items, then sent the final trade request up to me.

It was quite a distance, but I did see a small window pop up. This part was where keen knowledge and experience from years of playing VRMMOs came in handy.

The range of a trade window was a little over eight feet. But once you received the window, you could move another three before finalizing or refusing the offer. Faced with a small message that said *Alice has sent a trade request. Do you accept?* I stood up on the ceiling beam.

There was a hole easily large enough for a human to pass through in the roof just over my head. I grabbed the lip and did a pull-up. Just before I crossed that three-foot threshold, I let go of one hand and hit the ACCEPT button on the window before resuming my grip and pushing with all my power until I was fully out of the hole.

I knelt on the roof as a window appeared, saying *You have accepted 150 sawed aged spiral pine logs.* At that moment, a tremendous weight jolted me downward. I fell flat on my face on the sloped roof and tried desperately to keep from falling off.

The bear below noticed me up on the roof and growled deep and loud. The campfire was about to go out, but the light was just enough to see the large black form backing away to get a proper running start. It was lined up about three feet to the right of me.

Technique and knowledge were done. What I needed now was pure guts.

"*Nwaaaaa!*" I bellowed, just as loud as the bear, and extended my folded arms. I ignored the system message that said *Physique skill proficiency has risen to 3* and used all the willpower I possessed to shift my body to the right. Six inches...one foot...two feet...three feet.

"*Graoooorg!!*" it howled monstrously. The bear began a fifth charge at the cabin. From my precarious spot on the gabled roof, I could easily imagine being shaken and tumbling off, but I fended off that fear to bring up my menu. From there, I tapped the log icon in my inventory menu, selected the button to materialize, and jabbed OK with my index finger.

A number of logs suddenly appeared before my eyes, each one over a foot thick, and tumbled down the slope of the roof. They appeared in a continual stream, completely blocking my view. But I definitely heard the initial log slamming into the ground very clearly—as well as the scream of a trapped bear.

The spiral pine logs continued to burst to life before me, hurtling down the roof and leaping into thin air as they fell. And it was no wonder—there were 150 logs in our home storage space. Even the strongest strongman would be unable to so much as stand if he had all of that weight in his personal inventory. Making use of the trade window's range, however, allowed us to ferry them up to the rooftop like a bucket brigade.

The thudding continued unabated below, and eventually the bear stopped roaring. The modest-sized clearing was probably a mess of logs by now, but compared to the pain of losing our cabin, it wasn't a big deal at all to recover 150 logs...or a thousand, or ten thousand.

At last, the final log popped out of my inventory, rolled off the roof, and clattered to the pile below.

Suddenly, there was an unfamiliar musical fanfare in the air, grand and stately but somehow lonely, and a blue ring of light surrounded my body. It rotated rapidly and rose up above my head, then vanished, leaving behind a new message window.

Kirito's level has risen to 13.

From 1 straight to 13?! It boggled my mind. *Why so much?! Just for rolling a bunch of logs down a roof?!*

But a moment later, I realized the huge influx of experience points was not from the rolling of the logs, of course, but the death of the cave bear beneath them. I only wanted it to get hurt enough to run away, but the log fall was massive enough that it completely obliterated the bear's remaining hit points instead.

In that case, why didn't I get an item-acquisition message before the level-up fanfare? Even a wild animal monster should drop some kind of natural material, if not cold, hard coin.

Very carefully, I crawled down the slope of the roof so I could peer down at the clearing below. Then it became instantly clear why no items had dropped. I could see the bear's body, limbs splayed, beneath a chaotic sea of logs. Apparently, in this world, monsters did not disintegrate like in *SAO* when they died, but they remained as carcasses. In other words, if you wanted their raw materials, you had to get them yourself.

Assuming it wouldn't disappear for a while, I crawled back to the hole in the roof. Falling through it now would be the height of embarrassment, so I gingerly lowered my legs through, making my way safely back into the room with the help of the ceiling beams.

"You did it, Kirito!" cheered Asuna, hurtling toward me like a cannonball and throwing her arms around my neck. I patted her slender back and was going to tell her that it was thanks to her hard work, when I noticed the very meaningful glances that Alice and Leafa were throwing in our direction. With some on-the-spot recalculation, I said, "It was thanks to...e-everyone's hard work."

Alice nodded with a smug smile that said *Of course it was.*

The bear attack was the biggest disaster—well, second biggest, after crashing to earth with New Aincrad—since we'd teleported into this new world. But we'd managed to survive it, split up to recover all the logs in the mess outside, and returned them to the home storage. That left only the giant bear's corpse behind.

"So…what are we supposed to do with this?" Leafa asked uncertainly. Asuna and Alice looked at me. I thought Alice would have had experience making use of the wild animals she'd hunted in the Underworld…but I didn't want to rely on that. I readied my stone knife.

The graphics in *Unital Ring* were remarkable, but surely they wouldn't re-create dead bodies to a realistic degree. Surely they would make it as simple as a quick action or two to complete the process. *Surely*, I prayed as I pressed the knife to the bear's jaw. I swiped a clean cut from chest to stomach, and the huge bear flashed, then vanished, leaving behind many items.

As expected, a message appeared: *Dismantling skill gained. Proficiency has risen to 1.* I dismissed it and looked at the pile of materials on the ground. The soft, furry stuff had to be bear pelt, and the big pink globs were probably bear meat, but there were plenty of other little things scattered around.

"So they don't automatically go into your inventory," Asuna noted, scooping something up from the ground. It was a claw, large and curved, about four inches long.

Alice took notice and frowned. "But how do they determine who gets looting privileges?"

"Anyone can pick anything up…I'm assuming," I said, mulling this over. "But while bear pelts and bear meat are one thing, it seems like rare weapons and items dropping in a full-size raid battle would be utter chaos. Even if you decided on your rules ahead of time, there's nothing in the game itself that stops someone from ignoring them…"

It was a troubling idea to me, but not something we'd have to deal with for quite some time. Asuna tossed the bear claw to me and clapped her hands. "Well! We're the only ones here for now. Let's put Mr. Bear's guts into storage and get back to collecting the repair materials."

"Good idea," I agreed, opening the ring menu. Only one of the icons was its original color now. We had thirty minutes until the grace period ended.

Leafa looked rather gravely at the colors. "But, Kirito, we need to get iron next, right? Do you have any leads on where to get it?"

"I *may* have an idea."

"Oh really? Where were you thinking?"

The three women stared eagerly at me. I pinched the claw Asuna gave me between two fingers and spun it around.

"This guy's place."

6

"You know what this reminds me of…? *Shirodatsu*," said Lisbeth.

Silica paused and blinked, wooden spoon raised in her hand.

"*Sh…shirodatsu?* What is that?"

"Your family doesn't call it that, Silica? Um, you know, it's that stuff that's all squinchy and cruspy…"

"Squinchy. Cruspy."

Silica repeated the weird and definitely made-up adjectives, but they brought her no closer to understanding what Lisbeth was trying to reference.

In Silica's left hand was a bowl filled nearly to the top with a spicy-smelling soup. Its ingredients were just a tiny bit of shredded meat and a twisted, ropelike object that resembled pasta. It was no mystery ingredient, however—it was the crude whithergrass rope they'd worked so hard to weave.

Once she saw Lisbeth finish chewing, Silica scooped up some of the rope in her spoon, too. The rope had been chopped into pieces less than three inches long, but the way the woven material worked itself loose at the ends was anything but appealing. She hesitated a couple times before finally sticking it into her mouth.

The first sensation she experienced after biting down was a squishy resilience against her teeth, followed by a soggy crunch of fibrous texture. Now she knew what "squinchy and cruspy" meant. There wasn't much flavor to it—if anything, it was just the flavor of the broth it had absorbed—but the texture wasn't that strange, actually. In fact, she felt like she'd eaten something like this many times in the real world.

She tried to recall what it was as she chewed, and she found her sense of taste bringing up a distant memory. "Oh…! It's *niimoji*! I've eaten this at my grandpa's house way out in Saga!" she said.

Now it was Lisbeth's turn to look suspicious. "*Niimoji?* No, this is *shirodatsu*, obviously."

"I've never heard of that in my life. It's obviously *niimoji*."

The two glared and gnashed their teeth at each other, until the matter was settled by Yui, who was politely and cleanly chewing across the table from them.

"Liz, Silica, you're talking about the same food. *Shirodatsu* and *niimoji* are both regional names for taro stalk."

"Taro stalk…"

"Yes, the stalk of the tuber grown in eastern Asia. It is boiled and dried before it's cooked. I've never eaten it before, of course, so I wouldn't know how similar this whithergrass is to the real vegetable."

"Ohhh, taro stalk," said Lisbeth, staring closely at the boiled whithergrass on her spoon. "It's true that food in The Seed games all have their flavors and textures sampled from real-life things. I suppose, to create the taste of whithergrass, they must have gone with *shirodatsu*."

"You mean *niimoji*," Silica added, stuffing more whithergrass into her mouth. She bit through the fiber, then pulled the loose part out of her mouth with her fingers and lowered it toward Pina, who was sitting on her lap. The little dragon sniffed at it, then opened its mouth and ate the offering. Apparently, it wasn't opposed to the taste.

The group was sitting at the side of a circular tent about thirty feet across. They were far from the entrance and seated on a rug that had deep and luxurious fur, considered a seat of honor.

In the center of the tent—which was very similar to the gers built by Mongolian nomads—was a huge sunken hearth, in the middle of which was an equally massive iron pot on a fire. Seated in a circle around it were many Bashin tribe members, both adults and children, sharing a lively meal. The pot contained the very soup that Silica and Lisbeth were eating. When they'd presented the Bashin with the sixty whithergrass ropes as payment for shelter, the people were overjoyed and welcomed them for a meal. This was apparently quite an extravagant feast by their standards.

Silica finished her bowl, thinking that it wasn't that bad, once you got used to it. Just then, the spearman they met in the wasteland—who was not carrying his spear now—approached and said something in friendly tones.

"אאאאא."

As usual, she couldn't make out the words, but Yui was there to interpret.

"He asks if you would like more."

"Uh…"

She looked over at her partner. Lisbeth whispered "Maybe it's considered rude to refuse," so she went ahead and held out her bowl.

The spearman took it, smiled happily, said "אאאא, אאאאא," and walked back to the hearth.

"What did he say, Yui?"

"Um…," the AI girl murmured, a rare bit of hesitation on her part. Eventually, she said quietly, "He said that for a Fel girl, you eat quite a lot."

"I eat a lot…? When it was *his* suggestion…"

Meanwhile, Lisbeth was giggling gleefully, so Silica jabbed her with an elbow, then asked about an unfamiliar term. "Um… what's a Fel girl?"

"I don't know…It is not a word in my internal memory. I suspect that, like the Bashin tribe, it refers to an ethnic group within the setting of this world…"

Lisbeth downed the rest of the soup in her bowl and chewed the fibrous plant until it was gone. "So there are a bunch of other tribes of people in the world of *Unital Ring* aside from the Bashin, then. Maybe there's a more developed, larger city somewhere…something like the Town of Beginnings from Aincrad?"

"Oh, that makes sense," Silica agreed, looking up at the tent ceiling. It was made of thick fabric dyed with a simple pattern, and there was a hole over the hearth for the smoke to escape through that was star-shaped, for some reason. The pitch-black night sky was visible through the hole.

In the home of the Bashin tribe, there was this large tent and seven or eight smaller ones. It wasn't even enough of a settlement to call a village. At the edge of their encampment was a fenced-in area filled with goatlike animals, so perhaps they were more nomadic than simple settlers. In any case, it didn't seem likely that Silica and Lisbeth were going to find the equipment and information they needed here.

Of course, they could use the gear they'd brought from *ALO*, but according to Yui's estimates, the grace period where they could ignore the weight limits was ticking down with the changing of the menu icon color, with less than thirty minutes to go. After that, she'd have to put her familiar light armor and daggers into storage and change into something more lightweight, but at this rate, she'd have no choice but to wear her underwear. The Bashin women wore very cool and open clothes, however, so at least she wouldn't stand out.

"On the other hand…if there's a bigger town somewhere, I'm sure there will be monsters along the roadside," Silica mumbled.

Lisbeth mulled this over. "Well, of course. Man, four hours is way too short to have a grace period…We're going to spend all this time just building a shelter so we can safely log out. We won't be able to get new gear at all."

"It's a waste of the Blacksmithing skill you brought with you, Liz."

"*Sorry* that I put more effort into that than the Mace skill," Lisbeth said, sulking. Silica pinched the fleshy outer side of her upper arm.

"Not at all; I'll need you to make use of it!"

"Hey! No molesting me!"

As they bickered, the Bashin spearman came back with another steaming bowl heaping with *niimoji*—er, boiled whithergrass. She stuck her spoon into it.

The spearman then appeared to ask Lisbeth and Yui if they wanted more, too, now that they were done eating, but the girls politely declined. He nodded and was about to walk away when Yui asked him something.

"ᚾᚾᚾ, ᚾᚾᚾᚾᚾᚾ, ᚾᚾᚾᚾ?"

"ᚾᚾᚾᚾᚾ, ᚾᚾᚾᚾᚾᚾᚾᚾ."

As usual, the conversation just sounded like warbled noise. After trading comments a few times, the spearman spread his arms, then returned to the hearth area.

"What were you saying to him, Yui?" Lisbeth asked. The little girl looked down at her white dress.

"I asked if they had any extra armor—and if they could give us some."

"Wh-whoa…nice negotiation…"

"Actually, he said everything here at this camp is essential. Nothing is extra…but they will trade with us."

"The problem with trading is…," Silica mumbled, looking at herself.

Her inventory was emptied out the moment she teleported into this world. Silica's earthly possessions were merely a set of armor and her weapon, Issreidr. Even if they would soon be impossible to equip, she couldn't just hand those things over. And Pina, who was chomping away at a boiled whithergrass on her lap, was out of the question. Surely Lisbeth felt the same way about her own possessions.

But Yui shook her head and, to their surprise, said, "No, what they want is not your equipment, but your labor...or combat ability, actually."

"C-combat ability...?"

"Yes. The spearman—whose name is Tajil, I believe—says that, in addition to New Aincrad, which fell to the south, there was another small star they saw crash to earth to the northeast. They need to go investigate to make sure there are no demons riding on that star. If we offer to help them with that mission, they will give us weapons and armor."

"A small star...?"

Silica looked up through the hole in the tent. You could hardly see any stars through it. It probably wasn't a shooting star that the Bashin saw, but a piece of one of the floors of New Aincrad that split off when it fell.

She brought that idea up, but Lisbeth seemed skeptical. "We walked a long way to get here, right? Would a piece of New Aincrad really fall that far away?"

"Depending on the shape of the piece, I think it is possible," said Yui, hands clasped over the bit of her knees that stuck out from under the dress. "For one thing, Seed-based VRMMOs have a physics engine that sets air resistance to be higher than in reality. I suspect this is in order to ease the mental shock of falling from a great height, and thus keeping the AmuSphere's user-safety features from kicking in. But because of that, if it catches the wind right, even very large objects should be able to glide longer distances. It's just very rare for it to happen and might require player manipulation for a lasting effect..."

"Hmm..."

It was a difficult explanation to understand, but Silica mulled it over anyway and looked from Yui to Lisbeth. "Liz, if that piece of

New Aincrad had even a small town on it, we might be able to get some gear and consumable items."

"Well, I'm not going to completely rule out that possibility... but I think it's more likely to be part of a mountain or forest or something."

"Even so, we might be able to find some rare materials there that aren't found around here. And if we strike out, we're still getting gear for helping them investigate. There's no reason not to do it!"

"You can never pass on a good deal, can you?" Lisbeth said with exasperation, but she did seem to be coming around to the idea. "Well, I guess there's no better option available to us. Yui, can you tell...um, Tajil, was it? Tell him we're willing to help."

"I will!"

Yui got up and walked to the hearth to talk to the spearman. They traded words, and he looked at Silica and Lisbeth, grinned, and held up the cup in his hand. Silica felt relieved; the deal was done.

"אאא!"

Just then, there was a shout, and the hanging curtain at the entrance to the tent was violently thrown aside. Through the doorway came what was clearly the largest and most physically powerful of the Bashin they'd yet seen—and a woman.

She had leather armor around her chest and waist, but that was it. In addition to her considerable height, she exposed much more skin than the other women. Fierce, detailed war paint adorned her flesh. She strode forward to the hearth and spoke to the spearman in a husky but crisp and loud voice. Through their conversation, it was clear that she was of a higher status than him. The looks she threw toward the visitors from time to time were inflected with obvious hostility and disdain.

Eventually, the spearman shrugged and nodded. Yui came rushing back to tell the girls what had happened.

"That woman's name is Yzelma, and she is the leader of this

camp, apparently. Yzelma says that if you want to be in the scouting party, you should show your ability."

"A-ability…?"

Silica stood up, but she wasn't quite sure what to do now. Lisbeth whispered, "Maybe it's an event battle. If it is, this one's on you, Silica."

"Wh-what?! *Me?!*"

"I didn't even get to bring my weapon skill over. I only have Blacksmithing."

"Yeah, but I'm still only level-1!" Silica hissed back, but Lisbeth just grinned and patted her friend's shoulder.

If I'd known it would come to this, I would have done some leveling-up against the scorpions and camel spiders, Silica thought, but it was too late for that now. Anyway, the hours they spent between New Aincrad's fall and encountering the tribesmen were too focused on survival to leave any time for level grinding.

If I lose 30—no, 20 percent of my HP, I'll resign from the fight, she decided, handing Pina over to Yui. The little dragon flapped its wings to maintain balance as it settled on the girl's head and squeaked, "*Kyurrr!*" Yui balled her fists and added "Good luck!" while Lisbeth gave her a silent thumbs-up.

With her companions watching intently, Silica headed for the center of the tent.

The Bashin eating their meals backed away to the walls, leaving only Yzelma the warrior next to the hearth. Approaching made her size feel all the more real. In height alone, she was taller than Agil's giant gnome ax warrior.

Very belatedly, Silica wished that they could settle this with dialogue, but not only could they not understand each other, the grace period was going to end in less than ten minutes. She had to be dreaming to think she could beat Yzelma while immobilized from being weighed down.

Silica came to a stop across the hearth from the woman, who gave her a piercing examination. She did her best to stare back and noticed that Yzelma was not holding a weapon. Was she going to fight bare-handed? But just then, the woman bent down and picked up an extra log that hadn't yet been fed to the fire.

So she's going to fight with a piece of wood? Perhaps I should do the same, Silica thought, somewhat confused.

Yzelma stared keenly at her, then opened her mouth to speak. "ꓤꓤꓤꓤꓤ, ꓤꓤꓤꓤꓤꓤꓤ."

Yui promptly translated the statement. "Silica, she says she's going to throw the wood, and you have to cut it in two before it hits the ground!"

"Oh…th-that's all?" Silica replied without thinking. Yzelma couldn't have understood the meaning, but she seemed to have sensed something in Silica's expression. Her features sharpened. She shouted "ꓤꓤ!" and tossed the log high into the air.

Silica didn't need an interpreter to understand the challenge: *Do it if you can.*

Her right hand moved on its own, pulling Issreidr from her left hip. The piece of wood reached its peak and began to descend, spinning.

If she aimed accurately and sliced up from below, that would be enough to split it. But instead, Silica drew her familiar blade to her right side and flipped over her wrist. The blade began to glow red, whirring. Yzelma gasped and took a step back.

With the help of the game system, Silica's hand shot out over and over again, like a machine gun. It was the four-part dagger sword skill, Fad Edge.

The *Fad* in the name was a bit of creative license, intended to mean *capricious* or *on a whim*. Accordingly, its aim was slightly less than accurate, but through lots of experience, Silica had acquired the technique to correct it a bit. The attack's speed and power were excellent, and the dagger was an Ancient weapon from Jotunheim. *Zzka-ka-ka-ka!* The impacts rustled the walls of the tent, and the descending piece of wood momentarily stopped in midair.

Issreidr returned to its sheath in a blaze of light, making a little metal click as it slid in—right as the wood split silently into five pieces that fell into the ash of the hearth.

Before Yzelma could recover and say something, there was a raucous cheer from the walls of the tent, and the children rushed over to her. When they cried out "אא !אא!" with dazzling smiles, Silica suddenly felt a keen desire to learn how to speak Bashin very soon.

7

September 27th, 9:05 PM.

The end of the grace period came at last—all the icons on the ring menu were fully reddish-purple now. Asuna, Alice, Leafa, and I waited for the moment from the living room of our log cabin.

The last bits of blue in the system menu icon—a gear—at the upper left of the ring were slowly but surely fading, and then they were gone. In that moment, a series of events that I expected to happen, and some that I did not at all, occurred at once.

The first thing I noticed was the light coming through the window. It wasn't the rising sun. It was an abnormally brilliant reddish-purple color. I walked over to the broken window and looked out to see a series of rippling curtains of light in the night sky. It was an aurora.

Next, we heard a voice. It was a very strange voice, combining the youthfulness of a young girl with the thoughtful wisdom of a much older woman…but somehow, it felt familiar to me, like I'd heard it before.

"The seeds bud, sprout stems and leaves, and join ends to form a circular gate. Visitors to this land, drained of hope, preserve your solitary life. Withstand myriad trials, survive untold dangers, and

to the first to reach the land revealed by the heavenly light, all shall be given."

When the voice from on high died out, the aurora that lit up the night sky vanished with it.

Visitors? All shall be given…?

I pondered the meaning of the words as I stood at the window. But then there was a shriek behind me, and I spun around in alarm.

"What's—?" I started to say, until I saw what had happened. "I warned you to take them off…"

In the middle of the living room, three women were down on their hands and knees. Each one was trying desperately to get up, but the best they could do was keep themselves from falling flat on their faces. With the end of the four-hour grace period, the weight of their high-level armor was now fully applied and had over-encumbered them. Alice seemed especially strained, as the only one with metal armor. She lifted her face with great desperation and yelled, "Kirito, go outside for a bit!"

I was expecting this to happen, so I said "Yes, ma'am," and obeyed, carefully opening the door so it didn't pop out of the frame on my way out to the porch.

The impact of the thornspike cave bear had done further damage to the already miserable state of the log cabin. The largely unharmed front wall now had two massive craters in it, and the foundation was significantly tilted. The initial calculation was that we had until six o'clock tomorrow morning before the durability ran out, but now it was going to deplete two hours sooner. That meant we had seven hours until the deadline.

But there was reason for optimism, too. Out of all the materials we needed to repair the house, the seemingly toughest to acquire was iron ore, and we'd found quite a lot of it in the bear's cave. Apparently, taking in plenty of iron was how the creature grew those metallic bristles on its chest.

We used makeshift stone axes to chop out as much of the ore

as could be carried, but there was no way to know if this would make enough iron until we melted it. Which meant our next mission was the first real step toward the Iron Age—building a proper furnace for smelting.

"…But before that, I'd really like some clothes," I murmured, looking down at my avatar dressed in underwear and nothing else. I felt quite vulnerable walking in the woods at night like this, but we had to find the bear's cave while we could still make use of Leafa's sword. We did, in fact, end up in combat one more time while searching. It was a giant bat-type monster, and my brilliant sister was the one who ensured we were able to reach the spot where we found all that iron. Yes, I'd jumped all the way up to level-13, but in an RPG, it was your gear that truly defined you.

So the furnace came first and then armor—or at least clothes.

Then I heard a voice from inside calling out, "You can come back in, Big Brother!"

But that answer didn't tell me how they solved the encumbrance issue. Feeling skeptical, I opened the door carefully.

In the torchlit living room, the three girls were standing in a row. To my surprise, all three were wearing identical dresses.

"Uh…wh-what's with those?!" I asked, my index finger swaying back and forth from end to end.

With a look that was seven parts pride to three parts bashfulness, Asuna replied, "We made cloth out of the ubiquigrass fibers and turned that into clothes."

"Wh-when did you…?" I gaped. This time, it was Alice's turn to give me a grin.

"We already knew from your example that the equipment we brought over from Alfheim would eventually be unusable. So I started to prepare from that point onward."

"A-and were you going to make something for…?" I tried to ask, but Leafa clapped her hands to interrupt.

"Sorry, Kirito, we used up all the rough ubiquigrass cloth making our outfits. You'll have to wait a little longer for us to make more!"

"…Okay," I said, telling myself *I can always make it on my own.* There were plenty of other things to discuss at the moment, I supposed.

"…Anyway, about the…"

"Hold on, Big Brother. Don't you have something else to say first?" interrupted Leafa. She did a little spin for me, which caused me to snort.

"Ah yes. Of course. You all look very nice in your new—"

"Does this game have a photo feature, Kirito?" asked Asuna. Clearly, all three of them were quite pleased with their rough cloth dresses. Or maybe it was because, for the first time, they were all wearing matching outfits.

They seemed so happy that I *did* want to capture the moment, but alas.

"There doesn't seem to be a photography button in the UI… Perhaps there is a picture-taking item like in *SAO*, but I doubt we'll find it anytime soon," said the most crestfallen member of the trio, who, to my surprise, was Alice. But she recovered from her mood quickly to look out the window. "That voice from ear-lier…It was a very strange message. Something about *all shall be given.*"

"Oh! Yeah, it did say that!" Leafa cried.

Asuna added, "Saying *all* might as well be saying nothing…But at least I kind of understand what it is they want us to do…"

"The way it spoke reminded me of the pontifex," Alice said. At last, I smacked my fist into my palm. Maybe the reason it sounded so familiar was that it reminded me of the half-human, half-god master of the Underworld, Administrator, and her pompous, enigmatic speeches. Asuna and Leafa didn't seem confused by this, because they knew quite a lot about the history and events of the Underworld. Over there, they'd been the goddesses Stacia and Terraria, after all.

Of course, the voice just now did not belong to Administra-tor. She had perished on the top floor of Central Cathedral, her fluctlight obliterated. And it had cost the life of my best friend and strongest partner...

A sudden, surprising pain stung my chest, and I held my breath. Slow exhalation helped me sink that painful throb back to the depth of my memories. I smiled for the girls, who were looking at me with concern.

"Well...putting the voice aside for now, we should hurry on the house repairs. I'll go collect some stones by the river. You make more kindling wood from the..."

But I didn't get to finish that sentence. Not due to any external reason; I was suddenly overcome with a ferocious thirst, and I couldn't speak.

I looked below my HP and MP bars and saw that the blue TP (thirst points) bar was below its halfway point, and the yellow SP (stamina points) bar was also about 20 percent down. It wasn't just the carrying weight that the grace period was saving us from. It was also holding back hunger and thirst, and when that mysterious voice spoke, that protection vanished, too...From this point on, it was truly going to be a struggle for survival.

"I'm...thirsty..."

I looked down at the sound of the voice and saw that Leafa and the other two were also holding their throats and coughing. It was too early for our bodies to be getting dehydrated in the real world, so this was definitely a virtual sensation the game system was causing. In other words, we could ignore it with no ill effects on our physical bodies, but once the TP bar dropped to zero, our HP would go next. We needed to replenish our fluids if we wanted to survive here.

"I take it back. Let's *all* go to the river," I suggested, to unanimous agreement. Asuna, Alice, and I had our trusty stone knives, while Leafa equipped the stone ax we'd used to mine the ore, and we left the cabin.

With the torch in my other hand to light the way, we hurried southwest to the river. Just hearing its cool, rustling flow made the dryness in my throat feel twice as harsh. Initially, I expected to use some kind of material to make a cup, but I couldn't wait.

I knelt at the edge of the river, stuck the base of the torch between some rocks, and scooped up the water with both hands. It wasn't quite laceratingly cold, but it was still plenty chilly. As I lifted it to my mouth and gulped it greedily, a numbing sense of intoxication spread to the back of my head, and my TP bar began to recover. The girls knelt down to the sides and scooped up water for themselves. I repeated the process three times before I felt normal again.

When my TP bar was full again, I checked the clock in the corner of my vision. It was nine fifteen at night. I'd have to put up with the thirst after this point for a while and make sure I checked to see how many hours it took for my TP to drop dangerously low again.

Once we'd all drank our fill, the four of us stood up, then smiled bashfully as we noticed we'd all splashed water on our shirts, like little children.

"...I would like a cup," said Alice.

Asuna looked at the riverbank. "I don't think we can make cups out of grass. Maybe you can carve one out of wood..."

"It's probably easier to just bake one out of clay," I said. "Actually, hang on. It'll be a pain to come down to the river every time we're thirsty. We need to build a container that can store a lot of water—and canteens for carrying around..."

"What if we just dig a well, then?" Alice pointed out.

That made sense. Only Centoria had a proper water system in the Underworld. In rural villages and towns like Rulid and Zakkaria, people used wells and water jugs. That was possible because that world wasn't a 3D-constructed digital setting. But in a normal VR game, altering the landscape by making mountains and digging deep holes just wasn't possible.

"We can test that out later, but for now, the furnace comes—"

But before the word *first* could escape my lips, my stomach happily let out a tremendous gurgle. I felt a wave of hunger come over me, and now it was the SP bar that was nearly half-way gone.

The girls suddenly clutched their own stomachs, probably worried they would make similar sounds. That might have a helpful effect in the real world, but it would do nothing in the virtual realm…

"Aaah! Aaah! Aaah!" Leafa suddenly shouted. I flinched, feeling tense. At first, I was worried, but then I realized that it was her attempt to hide the sounds of gurgling. Ahhh, my sweet, foolish sister. As the big brother here, I needed to say a word.

"Look, who cares if your stomach gurgles a bit? For one thing, it's just your avatar—it's not you."

"I don't want to hear that from a guy dressed as a caveman!"

"H-hey, I'm not naked by choice. And you didn't bother to make clothes for me, so…"

There was another mysterious sound, and I fell silent. This time, it wasn't from my own stomach, but another source…A large splashing sound from about the middle of the river.

"…What was that?" Asuna asked.

Alice's face went hard. "Probably just a fish leaping out of the water."

"What? A fish? Let's catch it, then!" Leafa proclaimed, making no bother to hide her hunger as she approached the river. I grabbed her collar and yanked her back.

"Listen, we don't know it's a fish yet. It could be a crocodile."

"Ha-ha-ha! Since when can you find crocodiles in a coniferous forest?"

"And since when did commonsense rules from real life apply to a…?"

Splash, splash.

This time, the new sound was closer than before. Something was approaching.

"Get away from the water!" I said to the others at minimal volume, retreating from the river while still holding Leafa's collar. Then I picked up the nearby torch and held my knife in the other hand.

"Give me some of the fire, too!"

I turned left at that request to see Alice holding out a stick she must have picked up along the riverbank. It would have lower light and durability than a proper torch with dried grass tied around the end, but we needed all the visibility we could get right now. I leaned the torch over and lit the dead branch.

Now that our light was 50 percent brighter, it shone upon the blackness of the water. The waves were complex and churning because the river curved at that point, hiding whatever was under the surface. I waited for several seconds, but there was no new sound.

Maybe it really was a fish...

I had just relaxed at last, when the water burst forth just ten feet away. It revealed a round head and flat beak, just like a duck's. But this one was a foot wide and twice as long.

"...A p-platypus...?" Leafa whispered. As if it heard her, the creature opened its yellow bill.

"*Quack.*"

Well, it sounded exactly like a duck, but it wasn't enough to calm my nerves—because when that bill opened, it revealed many small, sharp fangs.

"*Quack-quack,*" it repeated, silly and nasal, and the massive bill began to glide toward the bank. I waved the others farther back. As with the bear, it did not yet have a visible cursor. It seemed that, in this game, an enemy cursor would not appear until you or a party member attacked or were attacked. In other words, you couldn't use the system's method of display to determine if a creature was approaching because it was hostile or if it was harmless and just wanted food.

The bill stopped again, just short of the water's edge. I waved the torch closer, still keeping my distance, but this one did not seem to be afraid of fire, either. The eyes on either side of its rounded head were black, reflecting the torch's orange light.

Suddenly, it broke the surface with a splash, and the owner of the bill rose up to reveal its body. The torso was squat, with thick limbs. It looked like a platypus at first, but rather than a furry hide, it was covered in green scales.

The platypus waddled a bit, then rose up onto its back legs. When standing, its head was level with my chest. Now I could see that its rear legs were bigger than the front and much stronger. Its tail was long and worked to keep its balance as it stood, just like…

"…A dinosaur!" I shouted without thinking.

The platypus (platysaur?) opened its bill. *"Quaaack!"*

It still sounded exactly like a duck, but those gleaming fangs were unquestionably carnivorous in nature and were going to do much more than hurt if they bit you. I was readying myself for battle, realizing that if it took one more step toward us, I needed to attack at once, or we were in trouble.

Just then, some kind of reddish blob flew from the left and landed smack-dab in the middle of the creature's open bill.

"Gwack!" the platysaur squawked, lowering its head and wriggling its bill furiously. When it had swallowed, it opened its mouth again.

I looked over and saw Asuna throwing another blob. It was about the size of a softball. At last, I recognized that she was throwing the thornspike cave bear meat at it.

The platysaur devoured the second hunk of meat and began to move toward Asuna across the sandy riverside. Its short arms waved, and it squealed, *"Quack-quack!"* It was clear that the creature was now begging for more, but I didn't know if feeding it more meat would satisfy it. The platysaur was smaller than the bear but twice the size of a large dog.

"Um, Asuna…"

I wanted to suggest throwing the next piece of meat farther, so we could escape while the platysaur ran after it. But she raised her hand to quiet me and whispered, "I can see a circular meter in front of it. It's about sixty percent full."

"A m-meter…?" I parroted back. Then it clicked—she was probably seeing a taming indicator.

It occurred to me that taming the creature would probably create its own difficulties…but I couldn't say that now. Asuna brought out a third chunk of bear meat from her inventory and was approaching the creature, holding it in her hand rather than throwing it. The platysaur squawked and briefly backed away, but its appetite won out, and it leaned its head forward. It sniffed at Asuna's hand with the nostrils at the end of its bill, then took the meat in its mouth and chewed.

Asuna looked at me with some consternation and said, "The meter's full, but nothing's happening…What should I do now?"

"Um, I don't know…"

You started it, Asuna! But the truth was, I wanted the taming to work out, too. I just couldn't figure out what the issue was.

Alice suggested, "When capturing wild dragons, we calm them first with meat, before putting the reins on them."

"Reins…? Oh, right."

I called up my ring menu and went to the inventory. There was something weird in the middle of the ring, but I was too busy to investigate now. I brought out the leftover ubiquigrass rope and tossed it to Asuna.

"Put that around its neck and tie it!"

The fencer—stone knifer?—looked intimidated by the thought. But I had to assume that the attempt would only work coming from Asuna, who could see the meter. She held the rope and slowly approached the platysaur. As it chewed on the bear meat in blissful ignorance, she slipped the end of the rope around its neck and tried to tie it into a knot.

"Th-the meter's shivering!" she said, trembling.

Leafa sent some encouragement her way. "You can do it, Asuna!"

"I'll tryyyy," she wailed, but the end of the rope slipped

through her fingers. Tying knots was one of the most difficult physical actions in a virtual setting, because of the fine coordination required between hands. In the meantime, the platysaur finished eating the meat and noticed the rope around its neck. It screeched, "*Quack!*"

But that was also when Asuna finished tying the rope. Instantly, the platysaur's entire body flashed, the same way the materials did when you crafted them into something else. The same 3D cursor combining a circular HP bar and sharp spindles appeared over its head. It was green.

"*Quah-wah-wah-wack!*" the platysaur exclaimed, rubbing the end of its bill against Asuna's face. Our first attempt at beast-taming was a success.

"You did it, Asuna!" cheered Leafa, throwing her arms around the platysaur's neck and scratching at its triangular scales. The tamed monster made little grunting noises of pleasure. I stared at the cursor, eager to find out what the creature's official name was. Underneath the HP bar was a string of words reading: *Long-billed Giant Agamid.*

What's an agamid?

I was going to ask Yui, until I remembered that our dear daughter was in a separate location. My next choice was to open a browser, but we couldn't do that, either. Well, the next time I logged out, I could do an Internet search…assuming I remembered.

At any rate, it was a very good thing we did not need to fight. Since Asuna successfully tamed it without having the Beast-Taming skill already, it probably wasn't that powerful of a monster, but we needed to avoid every possible fight until we had safely repaired our cabin.

"Okay, let's move those stones," I said, heading back for the riverbank to complete our original mission.

"Before that, we should eat," said Alice. My stomach promptly gurgled a response. It kind of sounded like the cry of the long-billed giant agamid.

*　　*　　*

We dined on a rather lopsided menu of seared bear meat, but it did recover my hunger and SP bar—plus the HP I'd lost from the fight with the bear, which was an unexpected bonus. Only then did we finally collect stones from the river. The other necessary materials were clay and dried grass. The grass was easy, but I wasn't sure where to get clay at first. Then I noticed the whitish spots on the ground near the river, dug them up, and tapped them to find that they were called rough gray clay, which seemed to fit the bill.

Once the materials were collected, we went back to the log cabin, and I opened my menu.

That was when I noticed, once again, that the inside of the ring menu, in between the eight icons, was no longer an empty space.

"Wh...what is this?"

This was a string of numbers that read *0000:01:03:24*. The rightmost digit was increasing by one each second, so I could surmise that the format was day : hour : minute : second, but what kind of time was it measuring?

"Oh, we noticed that when we were making the clothes," said Asuna, who opened her own menu. The same count was there, the numbers identical down to the second.

"Let's see...An hour and three minutes ago was...," I said, trying to count backward to the moment it started, but it wasn't necessary.

Over my shoulder, Alice announced with great certainty, "That clock began counting at 9:05...the moment the voice said *all shall be given.*"

"Oh, right...of course. But why do they need this counter? It's not like you'd need something like this to remember how many hours it's been since then..."

"If anything, I would have preferred a clock that says the real time on it," said Leafa. We all nodded. But given that we still didn't know who created *Unital Ring* or why they'd converted hundreds of thousands of players, it seemed pointless to guess whatever hidden purpose the UI contained.

"Let's just focus on our task for now," I said, pushing that frustration aside and tapping the SKILLS icon. From the list of craftable items under the Stoneworking skill, I selected *Stone Furnace.*

Something strange appeared before my eyes—a large, translucent light-purple object. It was a metalworking furnace in ghost-display mode. A new Tips window appeared in front of it.

Manipulating a construction object's position in ghost mode is done manually. Use pinch controls to approach or distance—and clench firmly to begin construction. Once in construction mode, it is impossible to cancel.

"Pinch controls...?" I repeated. I tried closing my hand a bit, and the temporary ghost image floated closer. If I uncurled my fingers, it moved farther away. Tilting my hand left or right allowed me to fine-tune the way it hugged the ground.

"Can you all see this, too?" I asked, and the three of them nodded. I guessed that making it impossible to cancel construction was supposed to prevent pranks or harassment using ghost objects. It would probably be fun to wave it around with my hand, but the last thing I needed was for someone to punish me with another open-hand slap on the back.

There was a decent amount of space in the clearing around the log cabin, but it was easy to envision running out of room if we didn't do this logically. After discussing with Asuna, we decided to get some distance away from the west wall of the cabin. I carefully adjusted its placement and clenched my right hand.

With a *da-thud!* a large object fell out of thin air and landed on the ground in the exact position of the ghost. Construction mode ended, and my Stoneworking skill increased again. The new object resembled a white stone fireplace with gray clay grout. The smokestack was about six feet tall, and a semicircular combustion chamber jutted out of the front like an oven. I couldn't tell how to work it just by looking at it.

The giant agamid approached it first, stuck its head into the oven area, sniffed, and remarked, "*Quack!*"

"By the way…what should we call him?" I asked the creature's owner, who mulled it over.

"Hmm…I'm not really good at coming up with names…"

"No kidding. Your avatar name is your real name."

She bopped me on the shoulder. "Yours is practically your real name, too! But…I'll think of something," she said, shrugging.

The giant agamid came trotting back, claws clicking, and she scratched him under the chin. Knowing her personality, she wouldn't want to just pick the first name that came to mind, but she would do her research and arrive at a name with meaning. That would require going back to the real world, but since she was borrowing her brother's secret connection to dive, she wasn't going to log out until we were done repairing the cabin.

"Kirito, let's use it already!" said Leafa, beckoning me to the furnace.

I walked over. "Sure."

I was expecting some trial and error, but in the end, running the furnace was simple. I tapped it to bring up a special window—and either dropped the materials there or transferred them directly from my inventory—and that was it.

The first thing I did was set a few of the ores we retrieved from the bear's cave, and following the advice on the Tips window, packed some wood into the combustion chamber. After lighting them with Alice's flint rocks, they began to burn nice and red.

The furnace worked like what they call a rocket stove, sucking in air from the entrance to the combustion chamber and shooting flames up out of the smokestack with a whooshing roar. It worked somewhat like a mini game, where you had to continually feed it more fuel at appropriate times to keep the inside of the furnace at the proper temperature.

I fed it log after log, watching the flames from the chimney, until eventually red-hot melted metal trickled out of the tap and flowed into a rectangular mold at the base of the furnace. Once it was full, it made that flashing effect again then vanished so that more molten metal could collect there. A message popped up saying *Smelting skill gained. Proficiency has risen to 1.* It felt like my character build was going further and further into crafting.

After three minutes or so, the flames automatically went out. When I opened the furnace's operation window again, there were four crude pig-iron ingot items in the completed area. I touched one to make it appear, tapped it gingerly with my fingertip until I was sure it was cold, then lifted it over my head.

"The Iron Age has arrived!" I announced, excited. It did not seem to register deeply with the women, who gave me a few polite claps out of courtesy. The giant agamid approached, sniffed the ingot a bit, then muttered "*Quek*" in what I registered as a mocking tone.

It took over thirty minutes and a hundred-plus logs to melt all the iron ore. We had plenty of spiral pine logs around, so the wood wasn't an issue, but the waiting was very tough, especially after I'd gotten used to the near-instantaneous crafting process of *SAO* and *ALO*. My companions went back to the river to get more clay, so I fed the logs in alone, and when it was all over, I felt more exhausted than elated.

Still, this meant we could move on to the next step. To repair the cabin, we needed iron sheets and iron nails, and to make *those*, we needed an anvil and a blacksmithing hammer.

For a moment, I was worried, thinking that in order to *make* an anvil, we would *need* an anvil, but according to the Tips window, it could be done with a piece of equipment called a casting table.

That could be made with the Stoneworking skill, but it required stone, clay, wood, and sand. So I had to go the river, too, and fill my inventory with rocks and sand and such. I felt like a kid in kindergarten playing with mud and stones.

I went into construction mode and created a casting-table ghost, then set it up on the left side of the smelting furnace. In the operation window, I set the production item to be an anvil, inserted the ingots and wood, and lit it up. The melted iron pooled in the mold, and when it was done, I had a crude anvil. I also gained the Metal-Casting skill, but at this point, my honest opinion was *Just combine this all into the Ironworking skill!*

The only remaining step was getting a blacksmithing hammer. That could also be crafted at the casting table, so I was all set to get started, when I was interrupted.

"Kirito, why don't you take a break from that and make us a bisque-firing kiln?" asked Asuna, who came back from the river with me.

I considered this for two seconds and then asked, "…What do you mean by take a break, exactly?"

"Take a break from working on the iron so you can work on some pottery-firing equipment instead," she said without batting an eye, then smiled. *This is what you get with people who take a break from their English homework to work on math homework*, I thought ruefully and opened up the Stoneworking skill again.

The bisque-firing kiln required lots of materials, too, but that was what Asuna and the others had brought from the river. I loaded up my inventory with stones and clay and such and went back into construction mode. At Asuna's request, I selected a location close to the cabin and watched them go to work.

The kiln looked like a gigantic dog kennel, with a door in the front and a combustion chamber below. If you opened the door, there were stone shelves inside, which they stacked with plates, bowls, and cups they'd made out of kneaded clay. We packed wood into the burning chamber, and Asuna lit it.

"My Pottery skill proficiency went up," she said happily. Noting that she was turning into a crafter rather than a fighter, too, I headed back for the Iron Age civilization I was building. According to my four status bars, my HP and MP were maxed out, while my TP was down 40 percent, and my SP was down 20. All that water I drank occurred at nine fifteen, and now it was eleven fifteen, so it took two hours for my TP to go down 40 percent. In other words, 10 percent every thirty minutes.

That was a very leisurely pace compared to the survival RPGs I'd played before, but that was probably subject to change based on the player's activity and environment. If you were engaged in heavy, continuous labor or situated in a baking desert, it would probably go down faster. Changes in stats, skills, and gear might make a difference, too.

"Hmm…"

I opened my ring menu. In the middle of the circle of icons, the mysterious counter was up to *0000:02:10:45*. A bit over two hours since that mysterious voice…but that alone didn't make me feel much of anything, except that time had passed quickly. I shrugged and opened the STATUS icon at the very top.

This strange *Unital Ring* game did not have numerical stats like Strength and Intelligence. Instead, it was more of a perk-based system—concrete abilities that could be earned, rather than increasing base stats. If a skill was a talent you practiced and built up, your abilities were the things you could do as a result of it. It seemed like the general breakdown was that skills were more for item crafting, while abilities were combat-focused.

At the bottom of the status window was a button to take you to a detailed screen for abilities, which appeared in a window when I pressed it. In the center of that screen were four icons arranged in a cross configuration. The one on the top was BRAWN, on the right was TOUGHNESS, on the bottom was SAGACITY, and on the left was SWIFTNESS. Two lines extended farther from there in each direction, leading to more icons. For example, BRAWN led to BONE BREAKER and STOUT, while TOUGHNESS led to PERSEVERANCE and ANTIVENOM, such that the farther you went, the more the ability tree developed outward. And each ability had ten ranks you could earn.

I'd defeated the ultra-hard thornspike cave bear by using the rare Rolling Logs Off the Roof to Crush It stat, boosting my level up to 13, so I now had twelve ability points to spend. I couldn't stand the idea of dying while I was saving up my points and potentially losing some of them due to a penalty. Spending them now was probably a wise decision, but I didn't see a re-spec button on the window to get all the points back. I had no idea what the best or most efficient choices were at this point.

In this sense, *SAO* had been a walk in the park—your only choices were between STR and AGI. I glanced over at the women feeding logs into the kiln and gave the topic some thought.

It seemed like we were going to be in the four-person party for a while, so it was probably best to consider abilities by distinct roles. If we kept our builds from *ALO*, I'd be a physical-based attacker, Alice would be a defense-focused tank, Leafa would be a multiskilled magic swordswoman, and Asuna would be a healer who could use her sword in a pinch. That probably meant I should take the Brawn tree…but in a survival game, nothing could be more survival-focused than Toughness. And it might be nice to learn some magic so that all my MP could be used for death prevention.

Plus, maybe the others would want to choose different roles than what they took in *ALO*. At this point in my life, I was finally learning that the secret to getting along with girls was consulting with them about everything, so I decided not to go off on my own selecting abilities and closed my window. I considered the freshly made anvil at my feet.

"Hmm, what was I supposed to do next…?"

Realizing that I was getting way too used to relying on Yui to remember things for me, I finally recalled that I was about to make my own blacksmithing hammer.

Once again, I faced the casting table and set the item to create. First, I melted down ingots to make a crude iron hammerhead, then combined it with a piece of wood to turn it into a crude blacksmithing hammer. At last, I was ready.

Next, I went to the anvil and set the ingots. In *SAO*, you had to put the metal into the furnace to get it red-hot before you struck it, but in *Unital Ring*, you could do it cold. I selected *Iron Sheet* from the anvil's menu and swung the hammer.

It made a high-pitched *clang!* and a message saying *Blacksmithing skill gained* appeared, but I was more concerned with the surprising volume of the impact.

Thinking back on it, the thornspike cave bear that attacked us could very well have been drawn by the sound of Leafa's sword skills slicing up the logs. Three hours had passed since that incident, so I supposed a new bear could have popped up from the same cave by now.

Asuna and the others looked nervously at me from the kiln, clearly worried about the same thing. I lifted the hammer in a gesture meant to reassure them that it was okay. If another bear attacked, we could still use the same log-dropping technique again…

But…no. It was too powerful of a method, being able to kill a much tougher monster without any exposure to damage. If the Cardinal System that was loaded into The Seed was managing *Unital Ring* like the other games, and all of its autonomous features were enabled, the system would have realized after the first use that the log-dropping trick was essentially a glitch and would come up with some way to prevent us from doing it again.

"Hmm…"

I looked from the pitch-black forest to the roof of the log cabin and back. Just in case the system only tried to prevent us from using logs, maybe it would be a good idea to stockpile a bunch of rocks. Or boulders.

"I'm going back to the river for a minute!" I said to the other three.

To my surprise, Asuna opened the door of the kiln, said "Oh, then take these!" and removed two round objects. Pots...? Ahhh yes, it was about time that my TP meter hit the halfway mark again.

"Got it!"

I trotted over, took the pots, and hurried to the river. I filled them up with water, put them back in my inventory, then filled the rest of my carrying capacity with big rocks.

Back in the clearing, the women had laid out the other pottery on the ground. Some of them had cracked during firing, but there were four cups, five bowls, and six plates that had survived intact.

"Here you go," I said, producing the water-filled jugs. Asuna smiled and held out a cup, which I took and filled with water. "Let's give this a try!"

I put my other hand on my waist and drained the cup in one go, refilling the TP meter. The others enjoyed their water, too, and we filled a bowl for the giant agamid to lap at with its tongue.

I exhaled and said, "So we have to drink water every two hours...This is going to make it really tough if you run out while in the middle of a dungeon or something..."

"What if it's like the Underworld, and there are sacred art...er, magic spells that produce water?" Alice asked.

I smirked initially, then said, "I suppose that's not out of the question. The real issue is how to learn the Magic skill..."

"Perhaps if you use it, you acquire it? Like with Weaving and Pottery," Alice suggested, then snapped her hand right in front of my nose. Out of pure reflex, I jolted backward, and she chuckled at me.

Leafa shook her head in dismay. "You're such a chicken, Kirito."

"N-no! I'm not!" I protested. *You just don't know how scary Alice the Integrity Knight was!* But I couldn't say that out loud. Instead, I drank another cup of water and handed it back to

Asuna. "If you have extra clay, make more pots and jugs. At this rate, there's nothing to be lost by having them filled up and sitting around."

"That's true. And it looks like getting the Pottery skill higher allows us to make bigger jugs. I'll keep at it."

"Thanks. I'll go make those sheets and nails."

"Good luck, Kirito."

We fist-bumped, and I headed back to the anvil. I just had to trust that if another bear came back for us, I could deal with it using all the rocks I had stuffed in my inventory.

I used a sliced piece of log for a chair and grabbed the blacksmithing hammer. It was probably just superstition, but Lisbeth the experienced blacksmith had told me that if you hesitated, the rate of failure was higher. So I put my all into the swing and smacked the ingot.

Clang! Clang! I put ten crisp, firm blows onto the ingot before it flashed white. It slowly changed shape atop the anvil and turned into ten thin sheets of metal. The repair required 216 sheets, which meant a minimum of twenty-two ingots with no mistakes. But even including the material for nails, I knew we had just enough. I told myself I'd be done with the iron materials by midnight and placed the second ingot on the anvil.

This was another simplistic, repetitive process, but compared to feeding wood into the furnace, it was much more fun. If I really did choose to play as a crafter in this game, I would much rather be a smith than a metalworker, I decided. But that would mean starting as an apprentice at Lisbeth's armory. I wondered if she and Silica and Yui were all right after falling with New Aincrad...

My thoughts wandered here and there as I worked, and before I knew it, I had 220 sheets of iron. Even if each one was less than a tenth of an inch, all stacked up they were a foot and a half tall. If I tried to pick up the entire thick stack of metal at once, the paperweight encumbrance icon appeared again. I was hoping that being level-13 would fix that, but at this rate, it was going to be a while before I could equip my trusty Blárkveld. I could carry it around in my inventory, except that my space was currently full of big rocks. If I got my weight down to half the capacity, I could lift the stack, and so I started trudging back to the cabin to put them in the home storage space there.

The others were busy kneading more clay in front of the kiln. It didn't seem like we'd need that many dishes to me, but I guessed they were serious about getting the Pottery skill high enough to make giant water jugs. Only one of them really needed that…but I was probably just being crude. They simply liked making dishes and utensils.

They waved at me with muddy hands, and I gave them a smile back, then headed up the half-destroyed porch. In order to open the door, I had to set down the stack of sheets on the floor, so I took the opportunity to stretch.

It was almost midnight, but I didn't feel sleepy yet. My nerves were probably just raw from being in this unfamiliar, dangerous situation, I thought, but then I realized that wasn't the entire story. A part of me, deep down, was enjoying this new challenge. There was an excitement associated with working your way through a new and unfamiliar world with no proven success strategies, figuring it out as you went along. Technically, we hadn't *gone* anywhere yet, just stayed close to the starting point, but if we didn't have the cabin here as a fixed base, I would probably have chosen to keep moving, onward and upward. Just like the time four years ago, when I'd left the Town of Beginnings alone, trying to reach the next destination before anyone else…

And because I was too lost in thoughts like this, I failed to notice it at first.

But I should have realized much earlier. I should have known that the clanging of the hammer late at night would bring other things than just bears.

"…Who's there?!"

*   *   *

Alice was the first to speak. I paused in the act of opening the cabin door to look at the cat-eared knight—and then in the direction she was facing.

A number of torches were approaching from the path that led southwest, toward the river. In the lead was a man of average height, wearing brown armor that looked like leather. The orange light source was reflected by the pommel of the longsword on his left hip. Like with the monsters, no cursor appeared just from meeting his gaze, so at the moment, there was no way to determine if this was a player, an NPC, or even a monster.

The group did not stop walking upon hearing Alice's voice. In a potential sign that they had no intention of fighting, the man in front raised his right hand to show there was nothing in it as he entered the clearing.

Asuna and Leafa took sides around Alice, and the giant agamid opened its bill in a threatening manner. I quickly leaped off the porch onto the ground. After making sure my stone knife was stuck into the back of my underwear waistband, I called out, "Stop right there!"

At last, the men came to a halt. Going by the light of the torches, there were eight of them in total. Twice as many as us…and they all had weapons. Some of them even had small plates of metal on their leather armor in a scale mail fashion. I was impressed that they'd reached this level of technique in the first eight hours of the game. The women here only had dresses made of woven grass fiber, and I was stuck in a measly pair of underpants.

They were checking out our tech level, too, based on the way they looked at the women. When the man in charge saw me, he went wide-eyed, and from the rear, I heard stifled giggles, as if in relief…or perhaps mockery. *That's minus one affinity point for you*, I thought.

"Are you players?" I asked, just to be sure.

The man in the leather nodded. "You too, I assume."

I didn't recognize his voice or his face. But of course I didn't. *Unital Ring* had converted over a hundred thousand VRMMO players. I couldn't tell if these players had come from New Aincrad or not—or if they were former *ALO* players at all—but I could guess that they'd appeared somewhere on this vast continent and followed the river until they found us.

As if to back up my conjecture, the man in the leather armor lifted his hands again. "We don't intend to fight you," he said, "we just want to rest a little. We've been on the move for nearly five hours now, and you're the first players we've met."

"The first? How do you have such a huge party, then?" I asked.

He blinked a few times, surprised, and asked, "What about you? Didn't you rush out of there?"

"Rush out…?"

I glanced at my other party members, but none of us knew where "there" was. I turned back to him and chose my words very carefully.

"…We fell here with our house. So you're the first players we've seen, too."

Now it was his turn to look skeptical. A smaller player dressed in cloth gear stepped forward and sized up our half-destroyed cabin. "I get it… You must have fallen all this way from New Aincrad."

"What? Is that even possible?" A large man in scale armor gaped. Though I had no evidence, my intuition told me that these three were the leaders of the group. The small man had a metal dagger at his left side, and the large man had a two-handed hammer on his back. Neither one looked very fancy, but they were clearly much stronger than the stone knives and axes we were equipped with.

The dagger-user looked up at the man in scale armor and waved his hand. "C'mon, old man, you saw all the wreckage from roofs and walls and such near where New Aincrad fell. I didn't see any houses that were intact, but that was hard ground there. If they fell on sand or water, maybe some stuff would have survived with damage like that?" he said, indicating the cabin.

"Don't call me 'old man,'" grunted the large man, prompting some brief laughs from the rest of the group.

Things seemed a bit more relaxed, but only for a moment—until Asuna said, "So you came from *ALO*, too, then?! Did you see where New Aincrad fell?!"

"Huh? Er…y-yeah, we did. In the distance, though."

"Where did it fall?! Is it still intact?!" she asked rapidly. The dagger-user tried to keep up and answer the questions, but the man in the leather armor put a hand on his shoulder.

"Now hang on…that's valuable map data. We can't just give it away for free."

Alice was about to say something, but Leafa quickly grabbed her dress and got her to stay quiet. I was sure it was going to be some insult about greedy small-mindedness, but it was the right move to stop her. I stepped forward and said to the man wearing leather armor, "All right. We can make a deal…What do you want in exchange for your map data?"

He turned around to confer with his companions for a little bit and came to a quick answer. "Food and a resting place…Preferably somewhere we can spend the night."

"Let us discuss that, too, then."

I lifted my hand, told them not to move, then headed over to the other three. The first thing I whispered was a question for Asuna.

"How much more bear meat do we have?"

"Plenty, but there are lots of them…If we cook a full, solid meal for us, them, and Aga, it'll probably use up all we have."

Really? I wanted to ask. *You're going to call it Aga?*

"What if we turn it into a soup, rather than cooking it directly?" I suggested instead.

"Oh, then we could make two meals out of it. But we don't have any salt or spices, so I can't predict how it will taste."

"They'll have to deal with it. Also…what about letting them inside?"

Irritated, Asuna briefly furrowed her brow, but she consented.

"That's fine; it's just one night. Well…are you okay with this deal, too, Alice and Leafa?"

"I suppose we have no better choice."

"Learning where to find New Aincrad is huge for us."

On top of that, the giant agamid quacked its assent, so I turned and walked toward the other party, giving them a quick nod.

"We'll give you a place to spend the night and enough food to refill your SP bars. But we don't have beds or blankets, and we can't guarantee the food will be tasty."

"Not a problem. It's enough just knowing we don't have to worry about mobs or NPC attacks. Logging out in this world is a major gamble."

"…What do you mean?" I asked.

The man in the leather armor shrugged. "You don't know…? Well, it's only been three hours. You heard that message, right?"

"Yeah."

"From that point on, whenever you log out, your avatar stays in its place, even inside your own home. If a mob attacks you, you'll be completely helpless. We basically came here looking for a safe place to sleep."

"…Your avatar…stays in place…," I repeated, looking down at my body. If I got attacked with zero defense like this, it didn't have to be a bear; even a fox or a tanuki—if such things were actually found in this forest—would easily kill me. If you didn't have a place guaranteed to be safe from a monster attack, or friends who would guard you for hours at a time, you couldn't even safely log out to go to bed.

"That's crazy…If you die from circumstances *that* unfair, no one's going to even want to keep playing this stupid game after that."

"Oh, that's not a big concern," said the man in leather armor. He, the dagger-user, and even the large one in scale armor, wore oddly strained smiles. He continued, "We didn't use this as a bargaining chip, so I'll tell you for free. In a way, *Unital Ring* is a re-creation of *SAO*."

"...What's that supposed to mean?"

Did he know I was an *SAO* Survivor? I was briefly nervous, but it turned out not to be the case. Instead, the man opened his ring menu and pointed at the time counter in the middle.

"You noticed they added this to the menu, right?"

"Y-yeah..."

"We didn't know what it was counting at first...until one of our friends got killed by an NPC. This is counting up how long we've survived so far. Once you die in this game, that's it...You can never log in again."

8

The party of eight, all men, raved as they downed bowls of Asuna's bear meat stew.

In the meantime, Asuna, Alice, Leafa, and I sat by the smelting furnace, poring over the map data from the man in the leather armor.

The problem was that there was apparently no means of directly sharing map data with another player, so instead, he'd used charcoal to draw on some cheap, crude paper. Still, it was enough to make out the features of the surrounding area.

The forest we'd fallen into with our log cabin extended an unknown distance to the north, but it also went another four and a half miles to the south. By following the river south through the forest, you eventually reached a short but treacherous mountain range that bounded its southern edge, on the other side of which was an arid wasteland. There was essentially no water out there, so if you left the river behind, you'd run out of hydration very soon.

The river branched to the west in the wasteland, and the men had originally tried to follow that tributary, but when they reached a basin with more plant life inside, they were attacked by NPCs bearing metal spears and axes. They couldn't communicate with them, so they had to run for their lives and lost two members of their party in the process.

To the south of the basin, it was even more desolate, and that was where New Aincrad had fallen. On a direct line from the edge of the forest, it was about six miles away. There was major damage to the flying castle, and the bottom twenty or thirty floors had been completely destroyed. The man in the leather armor swore that they hadn't seen any living players nearby.

That made me wonder if all the players who were stuck in New Aincrad when it fell had died on impact and been eternally shut out of the world of *Unital Ring*. But it wasn't the case, apparently; death being expulsion from the game only started after the mysterious voice gave its message and the timer started, after nine o'clock. So where did the players who died before that revive…?

Farther south from the highlands where New Aincrad fell, the terrain became grassland. Water and food were fairly plentiful, and he said there was a giant ruined city there. Apparently, that ruin, which was very similar to Alne, the capital city of Alfheim, was the official starting point for the players who'd been converted from *ALO*—and the spawn point if you died prior to nine AM. Just after five o'clock, when everything started, about four thousand *ALO* players (including a thousand-plus who died and came back to life when New Aincrad fell) were tossed into those ruins without a tutorial or explanation of any kind. The chaos and confusion had been extraordinary.

Nearly half the players logged off to avoid the chaos or to seek more information. The other half got to work figuring out where they were. They left the ruins, hunted small game, tried out elementary crafting, and built simple bases…until some players started to range farther out from the ruins in search of better materials. This party was one of the groups formed by those intrepid pioneers.

The smaller man with the dagger finished up their story for us.

"In open-world survival games like this, you can't just putz around with wood and stone at the start. Iron is crucial. You have to run for an area with iron ore in order to build a proper base… and that's an *iron*clad rule."

"Well…I suppose that wasn't the worst trade imaginable for our bear meat," said Leafa, causing Alice to giggle.

"Let's not be unbearable now."

"You get negative ten points for that pun."

Asuna smirked at that one, too, and examined the hand-drawn map once more. "If Liz's group crashed with New Aincrad and then revived, they would have gone back to these ruins, too. And that's a good…fifteen miles from here…"

I pointed at the map and cautioned, "Only on a straight line. It's at least eighteen following the river…But knowing Liz and Silica, I doubt they'd just sit around and behave at the starting point…"

"That's a good point," Asuna said. Alice and Leafa agreed.

Yui was accompanying Lisbeth and Silica, but our sweet daughter was not necessarily the careful and conservative type, either. If they'd left the ruins area, there was almost no chance we could run into them at random by searching. We'd have to make contact with them in the real world first.

Asuna realized the same thing. She stroked the sleeping agamid's head and announced, "I'm going to log off for a second to send another message to them and Yui. I want to draw this map on a real piece of paper and attach it to the e-mail, too, so it might take a few minutes. Watch my body and this little one here."

"All right. We'll take care of you," I said. Alice added, "Leave it to us," and Leafa commented, "See you soon!" Then Asuna rested her back against the smelting furnace, opened her ring menu, glanced at us again, then pressed the LOG OUT button. Her avatar closed its eyes and went limp. As the other players had said, it did not disappear.

"Hmm...I'm used to rotating log-outs in *ALO*, where your avatar stays behind," Leafa said, rubbing the giant agamid's head in Asuna's stead, "but this could last, like, ten hours at a time, while we're at school and stuff. Doesn't that put students at a major disadvantage playing this?"

"Students and people with jobs are at a disadvantage in every MMO," I pointed out.

For some reason, Alice gave me a sidelong glare. "I am neither a student nor an employee, but I do not have all day free to myself."

"W-well, of course. I know how abusive Rath can be to people..."

"Really? This is coming from the guy who wants to work at Rath?" Leafa snapped. I hunched my neck, and Alice gave me a very meaningful smile.

We couldn't really discuss or decide anything until Asuna came back, so I decided to resume my blacksmithing work. I put away the hand-drawn map we'd traded eight portions of bear soup for and got to my feet. The way she was leaned back against the furnace with her eyes closed, Asuna appeared to be sleeping, but I didn't have to worry about her waking up if I smacked the hammer right near her head. As for the giant agamid sleeping next to her...I could always apologize if it woke up.

With Alice and Leafa watching, I sat at the anvil, picked up the hammer, and twirled it in my fingers to look cool. Then I set the production menu to NAILS and readied a new ingot on the surface of the anvil...

"Um, pardon me," said a voice behind my back. I promptly stopped the forward motion of my arm, turned around on the log seat, and saw the dagger-user standing there with an empty bowl in his hand.

The two girls felt a little stiff to me, so I sent them a quick glance and got up, taking a few steps out to face the dagger-user.

"What is it?"

"Oh, I was just going to thank you for the meal. We've been eating bugs and rats and things on the way here. I've never tasted such good meat before," he said.

"I'm glad to hear it."

"What should we do with the dishes?"

"Just leave them on the ground."

"Got it."

He lifted the bowl and made to turn back around but stopped himself and faced me again. He stared at me piercingly through his long bangs.

"Hey…I apologize in advance if I'm wrong about this," he said, sounding hesitant, as though he couldn't believe what he was about to say, "but are you the runner-up from the *ALO* unified tournament they held back in February—Kirito?"

I stopped myself from denying it on reflex. I couldn't guarantee we'd never end up trading or otherwise exposing our player names to each other. If I denied it up front, I'd have to come up with an alias if necessary. And despite what I said to Asuna, I wasn't any good at coming up with names, either.

"Uh…well…yeah, that's me," I admitted.

The shorter man's face lit up. "Really?! Wow! I had a hunch when I first saw you…Sorry, do you mind if I shake your hand?!"

He strode over excitedly, which made it difficult for me to protest that I wasn't really big on things like that. I had no choice but to extend my hand.

The dagger-user took it in his own and shook up and down. The force of it caused the bowl to slip out of his left hand. It hit the ground and splintered to pieces with a great crash.

"Ohhh, I'm so sorry!" he wailed.

But at the same time, I felt a sensation that was both hot and cold, like a cramp but also like numbness. I looked down without a word to see a metal blade he had in his left hand, stabbed deep into my stomach.

*   *   *

"Kirito!" yelled Alice and Leafa. I had already pulled my hand free and retreated as quickly as I could. The dagger slipped from my stomach, the bright-red damage effects gleaming like threads on my skin.

I drew the stone knife from my back waistband and checked my HP bar. It had been full before but was now under half. One blow did all that?! I was stunned, but then again, I had zero armor on now, and the other man's dagger was a valuable metal weapon. If I hadn't gained all those levels, it would have killed me for sure.

The enemy expected that to happen, clearly. He narrowed his eyes with surprise and exclaimed, "No way. I got a clean hit in on you, but it only went down half...? Did you power level or something?"

I was under no obligation to tell him that I had. Instead, Alice and Leafa jumped out in front of me, brandishing their stone knife and ax.

"What was that for?!"

"You cheap coward!"

But the dagger-user was unaffected by the anti-PK squad. At last, a cursor appeared over his head, so I examined it.

Because he had attacked me, the spindles of the cursor were a deep ruby red. Beneath the slowly rotating HP bar was his character name: *Mocri*. I didn't recognize the name, but that didn't mean I'd never interacted with him before. Holding my left hand to the wound on my stomach, I demanded, "Are you with Laughing Coffin?"

Mocri the dagger-user blinked with surprise, then twitched his head to deny it. "N...no, no, I'm no historical big shot like that. I'm just a gamer, man."

"You didn't hesitate an instant when you stabbed me."

"No, no, no, I totally did. My heart was beating out of my chest."

Based on Mocri's mocking tone, I couldn't tell if he stabbed me as an act of treacherous role-playing or if he was a true pleasure killer like the people from Laughing Coffin. I wasn't as firmly anti-PK across the board as Alice; in games where PKing was a thing, it was the right of the player to engage in it, and if someone came after me, I was willing to fight back. But I wasn't going to get along with anyone who chose betrayal over cooperation in the midst of a strange, unprecedented situation like this.

The man in the leather armor and the rest of the group chatting enjoyably on the east side of the clearing noticed the situation at last, and they got to their feet and ran over this way. The eight of them must have been in a party together, because they all had red cursors over their heads now. Alice's and Leafa's were green, so red was probably the color of a criminal. Or…no, the concept of crime and law probably didn't exist here. It was just a regular old hostile classification.

"What the hell did you do, Mocri?!" shrieked the man in leather armor. The one in scale armor and the other five looked quite panicked. My initial reaction to this was to guess that Mocri's attack on me was an individual move on his part.

Then Mocri glanced at the man in leather and said, "Bolan, that's Kirito the spriggan! Second place from the tournament! And he's already crafting iron! Once he starts making swords and armor, we're in trouble, even with our numbers! We gotta kill him while he's still naked!"

The other seven promptly began to rumble and murmur. I had no idea people in general knew my name that well, but thinking about it now, coming in second in the central tournament of all nine races of *ALO* was like getting second place in *Gun Gale Online*'s Bullet of Bullets tournament. Any player who was interested in PvP combat would at least check out the names of who won…I supposed.

The man in the leather armor named Bolan gazed at me wide-eyed, then looked at Mocri and back.

"Well…I guess that settles that," he said.

"Whaaat?!" exclaimed Leafa. She jabbed a finger at Bolan's face and said, "No, it doesn't! Why is that a convincing argument?! We have no intention of fighting with you at all! He's the one who started attacking us!"

Bolan looked like he was searching for the right words. Eventually, he remarked, "You still don't get it."

"Don't get what?" Alice said, seething.

He shrugged. "This isn't just a simple survival game or some PK-friendly battle royale. We're being put to a race. What did the announcement say? *To the first…all shall be given.*"

"…And you know what *all* is in this case?" I asked him.

Bolan grimaced with chagrin. "No, I don't…but you can tell this is just as crazy as that *SAO* Incident, right? All the VRMMOs with decent name recognition—not just *ALO*, but *Asuka Empire* and *LunaSca* and *ApoDe* and *GGO*—and thousands upon thousands of players got converted into this place. And if you end up in first, you get something. Don't you want to know what that is?"

"Not to the point of killing total strangers," I retorted.

Bolan ran his fingers through his short hair. "Well, that's just your fault for being Kirito."

"Wh-what's that supposed to mean?"

"Any *ALO* player's going to know you're tough. A player like you, falling in this sheltered location with a house and everything? And with iron already acquired? Once you get your base set up and your gear together, you'll be unstoppable. But right now, you're a caveman with a rock for a weapon. Everyone can recognize this is the moment to take you out."

"You're being paranoid. We're only making iron to repair our cabin. I have zero interest in trampling over you to be the 'first' or whatever."

"Maybe not now, you don't. But what about when you're done repairing your house? You won't be interested in learning the secrets of this world?"

Bolan grinned and put a hand on his longsword. Alice and Leafa snapped into combat positions, and even the giant agamid growled behind us; apparently, it had woken up.

But Bolan didn't draw his weapon. He seemed to be very confident in their advantage.

"Luck is on our side. We were nobodies in *ALO*, not fit to lick your boots, but because of the equipment we brought over, we didn't hit the weight limit after the game's grace period ended. All the best players are wandering around the starting ruins with grass clothes and rocks for weapons, just like you. So we're going to make use of this advantage we've got," he announced, drawing his sword loudly. The steel blade was anything but "crude" as it gleamed in the firelight. The six men behind him had their weapons out, too.

If their gear came from *ALO*, that would explain how it could take out half of my HP in one hit. In a proper collision in battle, his sword would shatter my stone knife. The situation was heavily weighted against us, but it wasn't my style to give up and be killed without a fight. Alice and Leafa would certainly agree with me there.

Bolan didn't need to hear a statement to know our response. His face grew tense, and he barked, "Ten, Garth, kill the woman lying there. Doarn and Meito, get the cat-eared girl. Tetsuriki and Chap, the ponytail. Mocri and I will deal with Kirito."

They were clear and decisive orders from a natural leader. But I wasn't just standing around listening, either.

"Alice, Leafa, don't bother parrying. Focus on dodging and wait for an opening!" I said, just loud enough for them to hear. They replied promptly to indicate they understood. Lastly, I gave our final member some instruction. "Aga, protect Asuna!"

I had no idea if Asuna's pet agamid actually accepted my orders as given, but it did quack firmly in response. It wasn't a thornspike cave bear, but the long-billed giant agamid inhabited the same region, so it had to be a pretty tough monster, too. I wouldn't be surprised if its numerical stats were much higher than mine without any armor on. I had no choice but to trust it to protect its master from these players with the equipment they'd ported over.

"Raaaah!"

The enemy group, now split up into pairs, roared as they charged at us. Alice fled to the right, while Leafa took the left, and I stood my ground, awaiting the attack of Bolan in his leather armor and Mocri with his dagger.

Two against one in the open was a bad situation, so I wanted to lure them toward the forest around the clearing if possible, but I couldn't leave Asuna's side while she was logged out. No matter how powerful the giant agamid might be, its loyalty parameter was going to be at its lowest just after being tamed. I had to accept the possibility that it might turn and flee as soon as it got hurt.

"Hraah!"

Bolan came in with a deliberate yell and a swing of his sword. It probably *was* half for show, a way to grab my attention so Mocri could stab me from the side. Keeping the swift shanker in the corner of my eye to the right, I sidestepped the sword to the left. I tried to circle around to Bolan's back, but Mocri kept up persistently. So I changed course and made a hard right turn. Both Bolan and Mocri only had on light armor, but in terms of mobility, nothing was quicker than no armor at all.

As I expected, Mocri couldn't quite keep up, and I caught sight of his defenseless left side. I thrust out the stone knife and slashed his left arm. A few bits of red sprayed, and his circular HP bar lost about 5 percent. I wished I could use a sword skill, but the skill I inherited was One-Handed Sword, so I could only use basic skills with the knife.

My enemies, however, had no healing potions to use, I assumed, so if I could build up the damage on them, I had a chance of winning. I jumped back for distance, rather than going in deeper for more.

Mocri only temporarily faltered. When he regained balance, he glanced at his HP bar and the corner of his mouth curled upward.

"There's that second-place talent."

"Don't get distracted by your admiration," Bolan warned, but the other player just said "We're only getting started" and took another stance. I dropped my weight and readied for the next attack.

For now, Alice and Leafa hadn't suffered any major damage. The giant agamid's menacing bill was keeping Asuna's two attackers at bay. It had been about ten minutes since she logged off. The time was ripe for her to return.

"Yah!"

This time Mocri struck first. His smaller avatar leaned all the way forward into a charge that nearly scraped the ground. Bolan ran right behind him.

I couldn't avoid them by backing up. And if I jumped, Bolan could easily hit me in the air. My only choices were right or left. Last time, I moved left, so…*Right!*

Making full use of my near-zero equipment weight, I jumped right without any kind of preparatory motion. They wouldn't be able to keep up, and while Mocri was changing directions, I'd go after Bolan, I decided on the spot.

But when I was about to push off that foot, Mocri stuck out his left hand behind him, while still in his leaning posture, and Bolan grabbed it with his own left hand. That pulled Mocri into a sudden stop and swung him to the side. This extreme turn, impossible on his own, allowed the stabby one to continue rushing at me.

"Rrgh!"

I swiped with my free hand at the blade rushing up toward my stomach. My aim was for the side of it, of course, but it split my skin, which was enough to take another chunk of HP. I had 45 percent of my HP remaining.

Once again, I backed away and asked them, "You two didn't meet here, did you?"

"Not exactly. Mocri, Tetsuriki, and I go way back in *ALO*."

"That makes sense…"

Based on their teamwork without even eye contact, much less vocal cues, I had to bump my mental assessment of them up at least two levels. They called themselves nobodies, but they had a lot of experience and confidence in PvP as a team.

Mocri sensed my rising worry and smirked again. "Sorry, man, but we're gonna wrap this one up. I've got the hang of it by now."

"The hang of it…? That's kind of a vague thing to say."

"Well, that's just what Sensei teaches. Don't only look at one part of the opponent; grasp the whole. Then you'll know what they're aiming for—and what they don't like, you see."

"Sensei…?" I repeated, squinting.

Bolan smacked Mocri on the shoulder. "Hey."

"I know, I know. Let's do the thing now."

Mocri slid to the left, and Bolan drifted right, forming a triangle with me, each side being ten feet long. The dagger was readied low, and the sword was up high. Both of them began to shine brilliantly in the dark of night.

Sword skills!

If either of them hit me, I was going to die. And with them coming from both right and left, and high and low, the difficulty of completely dodging them rose significantly. The orthodox strategy here would be to take initiative and attack one of them first, but I couldn't use sword skills now. With a normal attack, my stone knife might easily shatter just from hitting their armor, much less weapons.

From all the adrenaline, it felt like my sense of time was elongated, such that I could feel the entire battlefield.

In the distance, Alice and Leafa were also trapped in triangle formations like me, targeted by sword skills from either side. All three of us were going to die together at this rate. We had to find a way to survive this moment and look for a chance to turn the tables. But how…?

"Quaaaaack!!"

At that moment, a high-pitched roar and some screams rose above the din. The giant agamid had bitten one of the men. The tips of Bolan's and Mocri's weapons twitched, and the glow of the pre-skill effect flickered. Instantly, I launched myself off the ground with all my power.

Of course, my adversaries wouldn't have been completely

taken aback by the possibility that I would charge *toward* them. But given my lack of armor, they had to consider it a very long shot. So their sword skills executed just a fraction of a second too late. It wasn't a significant gap of time in a PvE setting, but that could be enough to seal your fate in PvP.

"Nraaah!" "Chieee!"

Bolan's longsword skill Vertical came high from the right, and Mocri's dagger skill Canine thrust upward from below on the left. I leaped straight forward and twisted, curving myself like a high jumper.

The sword passed just over my throat as my head tilted back, and the dagger passed beneath my arched back, leaving me with only a brief chilly sensation. Aware that I'd lost a tiny fraction of my HP, I twisted twice before landing and immediately took off running. My target was one of the foes fighting Leafa. Not because she was my sister, but because she was six feet closer than Alice.

You're on your own this time, Alice! I thought, willing the words to her mind, as I sank my knife deep into the unprotected back of the enemy.

There was a foreboding cracking sensation. The durability of the knife, so abused by the bark-stripping process, had given out at last. But while the enemy was stunned, Leafa slid out of the trap they'd set up and headed with me to help Alice.

But we needn't have bothered.

Because standing there, knife sunk to the hilt into the side of one of the enemies attacking Alice, was Asuna.

"...Asuna!" Leafa exclaimed with surprise. I couldn't blame her; just three seconds ago, Asuna was leaning against the furnace in a logged-out state.

In the first second after coming back, she had grasped the situation, spent another second drawing her weapon and going into a run, and crossed ten yards to attack the unsuspecting enemy with the third. It was an incredible piece of pure reaction—but it came at a cost. Asuna's knife also failed to withstand the shock and crumbled to pieces.

Without missing a beat, Alice escaped her attackers and said, "This way!" We ran after her and wound up standing with our backs to the cabin wall. A moment later, the giant agamid joined us and purred, rubbing its head against Asuna.

It had fought hard to protect its master. Its green scales were torn here and there, and its proud bill was all cut and scraped. But after a gentle caress from Asuna, it lifted its head with brave determination.

The enemy group had been momentarily confused, but on Bolan's signal, they regrouped and formed a semicircle around us. They were done with taunting and closed in steadily from a distance of ten yards, swords and axes held before them. We'd injured some of them, but all eight were still in good fighting condition.

But on our side, only Leafa's stone ax and Alice's stone knife were left. Unfortunately, I had to admit that victory was even less likely than before. That left escape as our next best option, but if we fled, they'd take up shelter in our cabin and make it their base. I didn't know how the system ownership of the log cabin might be affected, but going by typical survival RPG rules, there was a good chance they'd officially take it over if they occupied it for a certain length of time.

To run or go down in defeat?

I couldn't pick either of those options. I bit my lip with agonized frustration.

"*Quee...?*" the giant agamid remarked with a questioning note in its voice.

Then something happened that I would never have predicted. A number of shapes jumped out from the woods behind Bolan's group.

I would have expected a respawned thornspike cave bear, but it was clearly not the case. They were thin and bipedal, obviously human. They weren't carrying any kind of light, so I couldn't identify them at all. There were six...no, seven of them. I could also see a very small shape behind them, like a child.

Bolan's group noticed the new visitors a moment later and turned around, pointing their weapons the other way.

A tall figure that I guessed was male, standing at the lead of this mystery group, lifted something long and thin like a spear and bellowed.

"ⵝⵝⵝⵝⵝ, ⵝⵝⵝⵝⵝⵝⵝⵝⵝ!!"

They were words…presumably. But muffled and distorted, like there were several layers of noise filtering over the voice, making it impossible to derive any meaning from them. Whatever the voice said, the figure's companions understood, fanning out to the sides of the spearman with axes and curved swords of their own.

Intuition told me these were NPCs, not players. That was quickly corroborated by Bolan's friends, who reacted with panic.

"Th-the natives from the basin!"

"What are they doing here?!"

"They're dangerous!"

If these NPCs were tough enough to scare Bolan's team with their inherited gear, they had to be the real deal. It was that very turn-the-tables moment I'd been hoping for—if we were lucky. But it probably wasn't going to work out that well. It would be too convenient to assume the NPCs would attack Bolan's group and leave us alone.

If there was a way to make use of this situation, it would be to launch a pincer attack the moment the NPCs struck, then run away as quickly as possible. I didn't foresee NPCs camping out in our player home, so as long as we came back before too long…

But once again, the situation swerved in a direction I did not anticipate.

Cla-cla-cla-cla-cla-cla-cla-clang! There was a rapid series of high-pitched metallic noises. It was coming from behind the group of NPCs. At first, I thought it was a brass gong or some similar tool to summon more companions, but the rhythm was too fast for that. It wasn't like an instrument, but an anvil or something, being smacked by a hammer…

"Anvil…," I murmured, realizing it *was* an anvil. Behind the row of NPCs, which Bolan called natives from the basin, was the furnace, casting table, and anvil that I'd built. One of the NPCs was striking my anvil.

But why? Just to make noise? Or was it a message to others, after all?

It was unsettling our opponents, who spoke among themselves in hoarse voices.

"What are they doing…? That's not good, is it?"

"Well, we can't just run away without anything to show for it. If we take this spot over, we can make new weapons and armor for everyone."

"What should we do, Bolan?"

After a brief silence, I heard Bolan say, "Tetsuriki, Chap, Doarn: Keep the NPCs at bay. But don't attack them. The other five of us will take out Kirito's group as quickly as possible."

Here we go.

I put my fists up, preparing for combat just as Bolan, Mocri, and three others turned on the spot.

The anvil striking sound had stopped, but no NPC reinforcements were coming out of the woods, and the six or seven of them were still standing there with their weapons up, nothing more. If they weren't going to attack, then nothing had really changed for us. Eight or five opponents, we were still at a major disadvantage.

I thought I heard a faint rustling from the woods to our right. Initially, I suspected one of our enemies was circling around through the trees, but there were still eight red cursors in the clearing with us. A bear would make more noise than what I was hearing, so it was probably some small animal instead. I ignored it and focused on the enemies ahead.

The group of five slowly closed the distance, their weapons at the ready. As soon as we were within range, they were going to launch into sword skills all at once. It was the ultimate orthodox move, no wrinkles—but that was what made it hard to counter.

The only trick I still had up my nonexistent sleeve was the stock of stones I had packed in my inventory, just under the carrying weight limit. Should I climb up onto the cabin roof and try the avalanche method again, while the others fought off the bad guys? No, that only worked on the bear because its actions were simplistic and predictable. The players would recognize what I was up to as soon as the rocks started to appear on the roof—and zip out of the way in time.

What to do? What to—?

"Use this, Papa!"

"——?!"

My breath caught in my throat at the voice that came from below. My eyes shot downward, and I saw a black-haired girl in a white dress covered by leather armor, crouching and looking up at me with big eyes. Eyes as black as the night sky, sparkling with stars.

"Yui?!" Asuna and I cried simultaneously, trying to pick up our daughter without thinking. She held up a hand to stop us, then used her other hand to make a gesture. I saw a small window that said *Yui has sent a trade request. Do you accept?*

A trade?! But Yui isn't supposed to have an inventory! I thought, shocked by this impossible request—but I hit the ACCEPT button on pure impulse. Up popped an error message that said *Not enough carrying capacity.* I'd have to do something with all those rocks to make the trade.

"Hey, what are they doing?!" yelled one of the enemies, noticing our trade window. An instant later, I heard Bolan shout, "Don't let them do that! Charge!"

Feet struck the ground. I didn't have time to organize my inventory. They would soon be upon us.

In a blink, I opened my ring menu and hit the SKILLS icon, slid my finger over, and selected *Stone Furnace* from the list of craftable items under the Stoneworking skill.

Immediately, there was a gigantic purple mass taking up the

space about ten feet in front of me: the ghost object indicator that I could use to place the furnace once it was crafted. I put my fingers together and spread them outward, sending the ghost sliding rapidly along the ground toward Bolan's group.

If any of them had experience doing larger construction, this wouldn't work. But since they were all using weapons they'd brought in from *ALO*, they probably had no need to build crafting equipment. So if my hope was accurate...

"Whoa, what the hell?!" Mocri wailed, toppling over in an attempt to avoid the ghost. The other four jumped out of the way to either side. I pinched my fingers inward to pull the ghost back, then sent it shooting out again. This time, Bolan pulled off a very impressive backflip to avoid it.

But of course, this kind of visual trick to cause chaos was not going to last very long.

"Hey, isn't that what shows up when you build something?!" one of them shouted, and Bolan's eyes and mouth opened briefly.

"Dammit!" he swore. "Stupid prank...That purple thing has no physical form, you guys! Ignore it and charge!"

Mocri and the others howled in response and regrouped near Bolan. They got their weapons ready and rushed us as one solid mass.

I moved my right hand again, placing the ghost in the space between them and us. They weren't dodging out of the way this time. If anything, they were running faster, charging headfirst toward the object they now knew was harmless.

And they were right. The *ghost* was harmless.

But just before Bolan made contact, I clenched my hand into a fist.

Da-thud! An enormous stone furnace fell into place right where the ghost was. A split second later, Bolan slammed directly into the thick stone wall, with the others piling against him immediately after. The impact was loud enough that the furnace shook. They bounced backward without a word and fell onto their backs.

I would have checked to see how much HP that had taken

off their cursors, if I had the time. The next few seconds would mean the difference between life and death.

I turned and accepted the trade offer from Yui, which I'd left open this whole time. Completing the furnace had consumed the majority of the stone in my inventory, and five new items promptly teleported into my now-spacious item storage. Their names were fine iron chest armor, fine iron waist armor, fine iron shin guards, fine iron gauntlets, and fine iron longsword.

Setting aside the immediate question of how Yui ended up with these things, I used the fastest finger speed possible—perhaps as fast as the time I once switched my skill and weapons to Dual Blades style when fighting the Gleameyes, boss of the seventy-fourth floor of Aincrad—to drop all these items onto my equipment mannequin.

Pale light surrounded my body, and the armor appeared on me. The design wasn't anything fancy, but the steel-blue metal had a deep shine that told me the adjective *fine* wasn't just for show. I didn't much go for metal armor that limited my mobility, but after spending hours exposed to the elements, the weight of this protection was reassuring on my skin.

Lastly, light shone on my left hip and took the form of a sword. I grabbed the sheath with my left hand and rested my right on Yui's head.

"Thank you, Yui. I'll take care of the rest."

"Yes, Papa!" she said with delight. I gave Asuna, Alice, and Leafa an eye signal and a firm nod.

"...I'll be right back!"

And then I was off like a shot. I drew my sword in a whirl and held it above my shoulder. The whirring sound of the sword skill warming up sent all the blood in my body into a feverish heat.

Up ahead, my five opponents were getting back to their feet after crashing into the new furnace. The axman closest to me gaped when he saw me. He started to shout something, but it was too late.

"Aaaah!" I howled, activating the charging skill Sonic Leap. A streak of light-green tore through the darkness toward my target's left shoulder.

Djunk! I felt hard feedback against my wrist, reminiscent of the sensation of the stone knife breaking, but the iron sword stayed utterly firm in transferring the full power of the sword skill. The axman flew backward, spraying red effects, and slammed against the ground. One hit took out over 80 percent of his HP.

A smaller shadow burst toward me from the left while I was immobilized following my big attack. It was quick and decisive, the action of someone used to fighting with sword skills. Mocri.

The dagger that stabbed me in the stomach minutes ago took on a yellow shine. That was the motion for the charging attack Rapid Bite.

"Shaaaa!"

Mocri zoomed forward. My delay wore off, but I didn't have time to use a sword skill in return. I couldn't evade it with footwork, either.

Instead, I let his dagger approach as far as possible, pointed right at my heart, and used the flat of my longsword blade to block the tip. My free hand pushed against the backside of the sword; this was a defensive technique known as a two-handed block that could diminish the power of an enemy sword skill.

Kshiannng! Two pieces of metal scraped against each other, and orange sparks burned the darkness. Blocking a big sword skill from a heavy two-handed weapon like this carried a real risk of ruining your weapon, but a dagger shouldn't be a problem.

The yellow light flickered, blinked, and went out…and I immediately swept Mocri's leg from under him with a swipe of my own. He lost his balance and threw his arms out in an attempt to keep from falling. From there, I set my sword flat at waist height on my left.

"I still owe you one!" I whispered, activating a new sword skill. Indigo light infused the humming blade as it swiped parallel with the ground and drove deep into Mocri's side. While there, it rotated ninety degrees and ripped up through his torso.

"Gaaah!"

Even without pain, the sensation of having your avatar's guts torn up was unbearable. Mocri groaned, but he had not yet paid enough of a price for abusing the rules of hospitality in an attempt to kill us all. After traveling from stomach to chest, my sword surged forward with explosive power. It was the three-part One-Handed Sword skill Savage Fulcrum.

Thrown backward by the force of the thrust, Mocri's body jettisoned a frightening amount of damage light and landed at the feet of Bolan and the rest, who were starting to run. His ring-shaped HP indicator rapidly diminished until it was gone.

I expected his body to remain, like the bear's, but I couldn't have predicted what happened next. The empty HP bar rotated rapidly, growing and growing until it turned into a string of numbers. The numerals *0000:03:02:45* clearly had the same format as the menu in the center of the ring. In other words, from the point Mocri heard the mysterious voice, and the true survival game began until his death, he survived for three hours, two minutes, and forty-five seconds.

The wheel of numbers stopped spinning and vanished, right as the sharp spindles that ran through the center of the cursor shot downward like bullets, piercing his body. The avatar dissolved into a multitude of rings that came apart in long ribbons, rising into the night sky.

Lastly, a large black cloth fell from above and landed with a heavy thump. That was probably his items and equipment. Bolan watched it with stunned disbelief, then his head shot up to glare at me. He pointed his longsword in my direction and shouted, "The rest of you, ignore the natives and surround Kirito! Do whatever it takes to kill him, if nothing else!"

The man in scale armor named Tetsuriki briefly hesitated, then bellowed and readied his weapon, the two-handed war hammer. He and his companions charged. The NPCs remained in their formation around the ironworking area and did not move.

There were six enemies left. Now that they were watching out for my sword skills, it would not be easy for me to beat them all on my own, but in order to protect Asuna, Alice, Leafa, and Yui, I had to do it. I'd have to avoid using big moves with long delays and whittle them down with regular attacks and quick skills instead. Once I beat their leader, victory would be in sight.

I took my stance, waiting for the six of them to reach me in their horizontal line.

And then, as though waiting for that very action—two shapes leaped forward past the NPCs and sprinted toward Bolan's group from behind, as quietly as they could. They'd been watching this entire time; why choose this moment to attack...? But a split second later, my suspicion turned to shock.

They weren't NPCs.

The people were dressed in simple leather gear, but the recognizable hairstyles, and most of all, the little dragon hovering over the head of one of them, were unmistakable. It was Lisbeth and Silica, who had fallen to earth with New Aincrad.

That explained the sound of the hammering earlier. It wasn't a signal; it was actual blacksmithing at work: Lisbeth had used my anvil, sheets, and ingots to make the armor and sword I was wearing now. Then she'd given them to Yui, who had used her small size to sneak around the forest to deliver them to me.

Silica got a bit of a lead on Lisbeth and smiled as she saw me. Now I didn't need to worry about holding back on the big skills. My two longtime companions could back me up.

"Hey!" Tetsuriki shouted as he finally realized there were two more people in the area. The instant I sensed that the formation had faltered, I held out my left hand and drew back the sword as far as I could with my right. A high-pitched whine filled the night, and deep-red light surged from the sword's tip.

The sound grew thicker, deepening into a metallic roar. The instant I sensed the system's movement adjustment kicking in, I leaped forward with all my strength.

It was the single-hit heavy attack Vorpal Strike.

Once in the air, I unleashed all my pent-up power. The tip of the sword barreled forward, sending a spear the color of blood toward Bolan's chest.

"Aaaaah!" he shrieked. Like I had a moment earlier, he turned his sword sideways in an attempt to block it. But the crimson spear shattered the thick weapon like glass and dug itself deep into his chest, past his leather guard.

After the loss of their leader and second-in-command, it did not take long for the enemy group to completely break down. I was going to let them go if they decided to run, but the way they chose to fight to the last man was admirable. Then again, maybe they weren't truly dedicated teammates. After all, the mysterious voice said *all shall be given* to *the first*, so even if their group had been successful, they were fated to kill one another in the end, no matter what.

The last one standing was Tetsuriki, the one with scale armor and the large hammer, but he was totally unable to keep up with Silica's quick, acrobatic movements and perished when she slammed a Rapid Bite into the back of his neck.

After the eighth bag of dropped items fell from the sky, I wasn't quite sure what to do next. I wanted to thank Lisbeth and Silica for their great help in the fight, I wanted to run over to Asuna where she held Yui at the side of the cabin, I wanted to compliment Alice and Leafa for their efforts, and I was curious about the NPCs still waiting on the west side of the clearing.

I decided the first priority should be confirming our safety.

With that in mind, I strode over to Silica as I put away my sword. The little dragon on her head spread its wings and cooed in greeting.

"Uh…so…Pina converted over, too, then," I said a bit awkwardly. Silica gave me a look that conveyed *Really? That's your first comment?* but it quickly turned into a smile.

"Yes. Liz brought over her favorite mace and blacksmithing hammer, but I only had my dagger…so I think Pina came over by being treated like an item."

"That makes me wonder if the cait sith dragon riders got to bring their mounts…"

"You know, that might be right. But dragons eat a lot of food, so I bet it would be tough to keep them fed," she said.

In the meantime, Lisbeth walked up and gave me a once-over, resting her chin in her hand. "Hmm. You look pretty good in metal armor."

"Oh yeah. You made this, huh? Thanks, Liz, you saved me."

"You can find a more material way to thank me in the near future."

"Uh…right…"

Asuna came over from the cabin, and I reached out to ruffle Yui's hair with both hands. The ticklish smile she gave me filled my heart with love, but there were so many questions to ask that I didn't even know where to start.

The girls hugged with tears in their eyes, while I stood nearby murmuring prompts like "Sooo, ummm, well…"

Eventually, Alice glanced at the NPCs behind us and asked, "Liz, are they not hostile to us?"

"Huh? Oh, they're fine. Those are the Bashin. Ever since Silica had a showdown with their chief, we've been on friendly terms."

"Wh-what? You make it sound like a manga about street delinquents," Leafa said.

Silica waved her hands in protest. "N-no, no, it wasn't some big showdown thing!"

"It practically was," Lisbeth insisted. She beckoned toward the five NPCs with their weapons raised. They spoke to each other for a moment, then slowly approached. It did not look like simple algorithmic behavior to me. They were probably high-level AIs, just like some of the special NPCs in the old *SAO* days.

Their spear-toting leader spoke to Yui, for some reason. As before, I couldn't make out what he was saying in the least.

"ⵝⵝⵝⵝⵝⵝ?"

"ⵝⵝ, ⵝⵝⵝⵝⵝⵝ," Yui replied in the same language. Everyone aside from Liz and Silica looked shocked by this. After a few more statements from each side, Yui switched back to Japanese to speak to me.

"So you fell here with the house?"

"Er…yeah, we did. The whole floor split off from the main body of New Aincrad…"

"Apparently, the Bashin saw the house falling from their settlement. They came here to discover what fell into the forest, and the three of us are helping them with that mission, in exchange for receiving some of their equipment."

"…Oh, I see…"

In other words, Yui, Silica, and Liz had crossed the wasteland to get here without knowing that they'd find Asuna and me. I had to thank the VR gods and the Bashin who escorted our friends here. I faced the spearman and hesitantly held out my hand.

"Th…thank you."

I didn't expect him to understand me, and he gave me a suspicious look, but he did eventually extend a rough, powerful hand to squeeze mine briefly before pulling away. That would have to do as far as signs of friendship for now.

But then I noticed something glinting on the chest of the Bashin man's well-worn leather armor. I squinted harder and saw, tied on a leather cord and fashioned into the shape of a tusk, a piece of glass.

"Oh…wh-where did you get that?!" I shouted, pointing at the necklace. The spearman glanced down at his chest, then smiled proudly and lifted up the cord to show me.

After peppering him with questions, aided by Yui's interpreting, I learned that the silica material used to make glass was on the highland across the river, and the secondary ingredient of wood ash could be acquired by burning any old plant. In fact, an examination of the spot where Alice lit our first campfire turned up a number of gray clumps. The stone furnace could be used to melt them down, so at least that second furnace I dropped in the middle of the clearing wasn't going to be a total waste of resources.

He also told me where the flax grew that we could harvest to make linseed oil. At last, we had a lead on all the different materials needed to repair the log cabin. After we thanked them, Asuna served more bear meat soup, which the Bashin ate with delight. It turned out that they considered thornspike cave bear the greatest of delicacies.

We saw the satisfied Bashin off as they returned to their settlement and then exhaled as a group. It was after one AM. We had a bit more than three hours to go before the cabin collapsed for good.

"There is still much to do," Alice said, clapping her hands.

Lisbeth bent and stretched her arm like she was doing warm-up exercises, then said in her usual energetic tone, "I'm so glad we were able to meet before the cabin fell apart! I'll make those iron sheets and nails and such. You worry about getting the other materials."

"Uh, s-sure…That's cool, but since you made the armor and sword for me, we might be a little short on iron ingots," I said, imagining that we'd have to go back to the bear cave for more ore or even melt down the new armor to recoup the material.

But Silica just grinned and pointed at the pile of sacks in the center of the clearing. "It's all right! If we melt down the gear those PKers dropped, I'm sure we'll get plenty of new iron!"

"…Ah. Yeah. That makes sense."

It was a very logical idea, but I still couldn't help but glance at Asuna, Alice, and Leafa with alarm.

9

"Yawwwn..."

As soon as she realized class would be over in just five more minutes, Asuna Yuuki felt yet another wave of fatigue crash over her.

It was twelve forty-five on Monday, September 28th. The specialty high school that Asuna attended, colloquially known as returnee school, started on the late side, with its first period at nine AM. That was helpful for her, because of her long commute, but it also meant that fourth period ended that much later, and it was a test of her wakefulness on days when she was short on sleep.

Asuna lived in the neighborhood of Miyasaka in Setagaya Ward. The closest train station was Miyanosaka, where she took the Setagaya Line to Shimo-Takaido, followed by a single-station trip on the Keio Line to Meidaimae, then a switch to the Inokashira Line to Kichijoji Station, where she took a bus to the school campus in Nishitokyo at last. Kazuto had told her it was "only thirty minutes by motorcycle," which she laughed off as a joke, but lately she was taking the idea more and more seriously.

Of course, her parents wouldn't allow her to get a motorcycle license. And long-distance commuting wasn't that bad if she considered it a part of her rehabilitation, but only when she was in good condition. Yesterday—well, this morning—she stayed up until five o'clock and only slept for an hour and a half, so she had zoned out on the train and nearly missed the first station where she needed to switch lines. She had no choice but to put on her Augma so Yui could give her regular wake-up alarms. Ultimately, she started coming up with Kazuto-like daydreams, like wishing that Yui could autopilot her physical body until it got to school.

While in class, she had to fight desperately against the repeated assault of sleepiness, but she had no regrets. It was worth the trouble; the full repair of their log cabin had seemed impossible at one point, but they'd gotten it done.

At this moment, their avatars were resting in the living room of their restored cabin. That was because of *Unital Ring*'s bizarre choice to keep their avatars present in the world while logged out, but at the very least, it seemed that unrelated players couldn't break into a home—Lisbeth tried it as a test before she joined the official party. There was no worry of unknown strangers killing their lifeless avatars while they were away.

But that didn't mean they were totally safe. The log cabin itself was not an indestructible object. According to Kazuto, it was probably vulnerable to explosives, catapults, and attacks from large monsters. At the moment, Aga the long-billed giant agamid and Yui were guarding the cabin, but if someone attacked, she and Kazuto had no means of fighting back without diving in from school.

So before they logged out this morning, the group decided on a new goal: building as sturdy of a wall as possible around the cabin and taming more monsters to protect it. They wanted more crafting equipment as well, and that involved acquiring tons of resources. There were so many things to do, she wanted to just rush home, stick the AmuSphere on her head, and lie down on her bed.

I always swore to myself that I'd keep my VRMMO commitment to a responsible level. And here I am, as swept up as I've ever been.

She was just smirking to herself with chagrin when a classical music chime signaled the end of class.

Asuna stood up and bowed with her classmates. Once the teacher left the front door of the classroom, the air in the room relaxed, like always. But this time, it felt like there was a faint tension and excitement in the mix. She looked around and saw that the students who admitted they were VRMMO players had grouped up into little circles, muttering and whispering among themselves. They all had to be trading information about *Unital Ring* after being absorbed into the game.

Asuna was supposed to meet up with Rika, Keiko, and Kazuto at the cafeteria during lunch to discuss their next steps, too. They were going to use Augmas to bring Suguha and Shino the *GGO* player into their discussion, as they went to different schools.

Sinon had accounts in both *GGO* and *ALO*, but it was her main *GGO* account that had been converted. They hadn't been able to contact her yesterday, either, because she'd gotten spat out somewhere in the game world and went through an adventure of her own. Asuna would get to hear about it today.

The Internet was ablaze with the topic, and the wiki sites were in total chaos, but Yui was sifting through tons of information for them. She was upset that she was treated like a normal player without any special privileges now, but to tell the truth, Asuna was just a little bit happy about it. Her daughter had saved them so many times up to this point, and now Asuna would have the chance to protect Yui instead.

Having HP meant she could die. But they'd never let anyone harm her. Asuna would do whatever it took to keep Yui safe until the abnormality was over, and they could return to Alfheim… or until they reached what the mysterious voice called the land revealed by the heavenly light.

Ready to head to the cafeteria with renewed determination, Asuna started to get up from her desk—but someone was standing before her.

The person said, "Are you…Asuna Yuuki?"

"...?"

Asuna looked up and saw a girl looking down at her with a hint of a smile. She didn't know this student. And in fact, the gray blazer with dark-blue lapels didn't even belong to the returnee school.

The girl's hair was as long as Asuna's and as black and glossy as crow feathers. Her skin was as pale as snow, and her features were so pristine and delicate that Asuna could almost feel the chill of ice emanating from them.

"Yes, that's me...," Asuna said, standing up. "Who are you?"

The girl was about Asuna's height. She bowed and said, "It's nice to meet you. I'm Shikimi Kamura...I transferred here just today. I'm looking forward to getting to know you."

—~∿~—

"Fwahuawh......"

I yawned tremendously and dug into my uniform pocket. In it was the eye-drop bottle I brought from home. I popped off the cap and was about to tilt it upside down toward my eye when I felt another yawn rising to escape.

In the old *SAO* days, I could hunt until morning, nap for two or three hours, then go back to fighting like it was nothing. And now after one measly night of hard work, I was a total wreck. I'd grown soft. I blinked and blinked again, waiting for the sleepiness to pass.

It was finally lunch break, and the classroom was buzzing a bit more than on your typical Monday. There were more than a few VRMMO players in the class, and they were all talking about the *UR* incident in hushed tones. It only made sense. Over twenty hours had passed since the mass conversion happened, and the cause was still unexplained. Ymir and all the other developers had only announced that they were "investigating."

Of course, I had no way of knowing what had happened, either. But there was one guess on my mind. If there was any human

being capable of pulling off an unbelievable feat like unifying all The Seed Nexus worlds, it would be the man who created The Seed Package and its predecessor, the Cardinal System: Akihiko Kayaba.

Technically, Kayaba was no longer a human being. He had performed a high-resolution scan of his own fluctlight in a prototype STL, frying his brain and killing himself in the process...but his consciousness still lurked somewhere out there on the networks of the world as computer code. Yui was always on the lookout, but she'd only ever found trace evidence of his presence.

Did Kayaba's ghost cause the *Unital Ring* incident? And if so, why...?

I considered this topic several times during class, but that question was always the dead end that stopped me. I clenched my eyes shut, then remembered that I was still holding the dropper and lifted my face.

"I'll drip 'em for ya," said a voice just in front of my desk. Without opening my eyes, I held out the bottle and said, "Sure...thanks."

Fingertips brushed mine as they took the container. Then they pulled the lid of my right eye back, and the tube right before my eye let loose a clear droplet. The process repeated for my left eye.

I squeezed my eyes shut against the powerful sensation and let my brain work again. Who was out there? I knew I'd heard that voice before, but it wasn't Lisbeth or Silica or Asuna, and it certainly wasn't Suguha or Sinon, because they didn't go to this school. The stinging was finally wearing off, so I opened my eyes and caught sight of the mystery person with, once again, clear vision.

It was a shorter student. She was wearing a black sailor-style uniform top that didn't belong to this school, with a khaki-brown jacket. Her hair was a short bob with the color a bit bleached out. Her face was...kind of familiar but not really...

"Um...who are you...?" I asked, unsure.

The girl rolled her neck and shrugged in annoyance. "Awww, c'mon. That's not cool. I finally got transferred here, and you don't even remember Big Sis?"

That strange, distinct way of speaking. Casual but with a nasal twist.

Wait. Wait...wait.

"Huh? Hang on...But..."

I started to rise from my seat, and the girl pulled the hood of her jacket over her head, then used her fingertips to draw a series of three lines on her right cheek.

"Ah...aaaaaah!!"

I yelped awkwardly with understanding the moment it clicked. The classroom went quiet. I could feel the stares of my classmates on me, but I couldn't possibly pay attention to them now.

"A-Argo...?! Is that you?! Why...? How...?!"

You're alive! I wanted to say, but my mouth just opened and shut without noise.

With a mischievous grin, the elite information dealer known as Argo the Rat, who once held all the information of Aincrad under her thumb said, "It's been a while, Kiri-boy."

(To be continued)

AFTERWORD

Thank you for reading *Sword Art Online 21: Unital Ring I*!

As of *Moon Cradle*, the previous story arc, I have completely run through all the material previously published on my website, so from this volume onward, *SAO* is officially in uncharted territory, both for you readers and for me. Technically, *Progressive* is also new material, but it's also taking place in the past. In other words, ten years after the end of my web serialization of *SAO*, time is finally moving forward in the story. The *Unital Ring* arc starts on September 27th, 2026, which is about a month after the end of the *Alicization* arc. In three days, it will be Asuna's nineteenth birthday, and one week after that will be Kirito's eighteenth. When you consider that they were both in middle school at the time they met on the first floor of Aincrad, it really does make you think "Wow, time's really flown by..."

While this might be the first wholly new work in the series in a decade, the key word of *Unification* in this volume is a development that I've had planned since the point I introduced the concept of The Seed back in the *Fairy Dance* arc. I had some hazy ideas about what kind of game world would exist after the Unification (such as the focus on crafting or needing to eat to avoid starvation) but the emergence of the open-world survival genre in the past ten years gave me lots of terminology to borrow. I haven't actually played any of those games yet, but once I'm done with this book, I'd like to try one out. Now that I think about it, the only game I've dedicated serious time to this year is *Fatal Bullet*…

As a story about starting over from the beginning, this one involved Kirito and friends figuring out what to do by trial and error without any help. I also introduced two suspicious new characters at the end, so I think the next volume should dig a little deeper into what the game world actually is. Maybe we'll even see some of the characters who only got name-dropped in this volume, like Kikuoka and Agil, or others who didn't get mentioned at all, like Klein…

I'd give you an update on my personal life…but I haven't done anything but work for so long, I have nothing new to share (*cries*). But at least the *Alicization* anime has started, so I've got a huge source of energy charging my batteries every week. It's scheduled to be a four-cour series, so I hope you're all ready for a long haul!

Because of the pressure of writing a totally new story for the first time in ten years, the production of this book behind the scenes was more thrilling than ever before. Unfortunately, I caused plenty of trouble for my editors Miki and Adachi, the proofreaders, and the printing company. I forced abec to produce those wonderful illustrations on an insanely tight schedule. I'm so sorry. One of these days I'll apologize in material terms! And now, I hope I'll see you again in the next volume!

Reki Kawahara—October 2018